Angelina Beac…

Book One of the Angelina Beacon Series

BY: SANDY THRUSH

ILLUSTRATED BY: BETH CLEMENTS

For Cheri. . .here's a story, "out loud", just for you.

I Love You

Sandy

To Kayla –
Enjoy High School!
Grandma –
Sandy Thrush
9/10/09

Just-For-Fun Publishing, LLC
Kentwood, Michigan
~2009~

Published by Just-For-Fun Publishing, LLC
PO Box 888162, Kentwood, MI 49588-8162.

Print production by: BP: bang printing
Brainerd, MN

Cover production by: Sadie Cross, BRIOprint, LLC,
Minneapolis, MN

Illustrations by: Beth Clements
Greenville, MI

Just-For-Fun Publishing books may be purchased in bulk for educational, business, fundraising, or sales promotional use. For information, please email sandy@justforfunpublishing.com or visit our web site at www.justforfunpublishing.com.

Publisher's Note: This story is a work of fiction. Names, characters, places, are products of the author's imagination or are used fictitiously. No characters or incidents are drawn from real people or real incidents.

ISBN 978-0-9821371-2-3

Contents

ANGELINA BEACON'S SECRET

CHAPTER ONE

DID YOU SAY THAT OUT LOUD?

Angelina sat so her arm shielded the top of her desk. Slowly the pencil spun clockwise in front of her. Glancing up to be sure Mr. Crawford's back was still to the class; she made the pencil lift half an inch off the desktop. As she watched it continue to spin in midair, she was acutely aware of Jordan Bradford. He was sitting in the back row, not paying attention to Mr. Crawford's detailed explanation of the Algebra equation. Instead, he was thinking about the new Flight Masters video game at Baker's Books & Stuff that he wanted so badly he was actually considering shoplifting it. *He's thinking of doing it tonight.*

Angelina let the pencil fall and turned her head to look back at him. Jordan raised his head to find her staring at him. Ever so slightly she shook her head.

Oh no. She knows I'm going to lift the video game tonight from Baker's. Naw. That's silly. How can she possibly know what I'm going to do? Angelina slowly nodded her head at him. Jordan's face paled as he stared back at her, a weird tingling sensation running up and down his spine. This wasn't the first time he had the feeling that she knew what he was thinking. She winked at him and turned back to face the front of the class.

Angelina reached over and caught her pencil just as it rolled off the edge of her desk. Mr. Crawford's monotone voice droned on as he continued explaining the Algebra equation. Suddenly, he stopped writing on the board. *Drat! Why do I keep making the same mistake?* He reached in frustration for the eraser. Grinning, Angelina made the eraser slide just out of his reach. His hand came down hard on the tray and chalk dust wafted up into the air dusting the front of his brown slacks. *Great, this is just perfect.* A loud sigh escaped his lips as his head jerked to look for the eraser.

Quickly erasing his mistake, he set the eraser down and picked up the chalk to redo the equation. Ever so slightly, Angelina pushed his hand so a long line messed up his equation. Covering her mouth to stifle a giggle, she watched as Mr. Crawford's back stiffened. He reached once more for the eraser that again she moved just out of his each. He jerked his head around as once again chalk dust filled the air. His beady little eyes, almost hidden behind the small round glasses riding on the end of his nose, squinted in frustration as he scanned the class. *Why, only in THIS class, do these weird things happen?*

The sudden ringing of the bell announced the end of class, drowning out the snickers of the students. Brushing the front of his pants, Mr. Crawford barked out over the rising noise that the problems at the end of the chapter were due the next day. Since Thursday was midterms, they would spend tomorrow, Wednesday, reviewing.

Amid the shoving in of chairs and general laughter,

Mr. Crawford volunteered, "If any of you still do not understand the equation, you may come and see me during fifth period." Angelina slowly walked up to the front of the class, paused to stare at the blackboard, and then pointed to the long line. "Is *that* part of the equation?" she asked. Mr. Crawford's eyes narrowed as he looked at her. *Is she serious, or just being a smart aleck?* He cleared his throat before answering, "No, Miss Beacon, it is not part of the equation. My hand slipped while I was writing." Angelina's right eyebrow rose, "Oh, it *slipped*, h-m-m?" Nodding her head and giving a slight shrug, she turned and walked out of the classroom.

Mr. Crawford followed her to the door and watched her walk down the hall. *She sure is one strange girl.* Grinning, Angelina turned and smiled at Mr. Crawford. He stumbled backward and nearly fell trying to get back into the room.

Jordan, who had watched the whole exchange from across the hall, turned and followed Angelina to their next class. Shaking his head and grinning, he thought; *there's something very strange about that girl.*

Angelina slowed her pace so Jordan would catch up with her; she turned her head just as he reached her and smiled.

"How do you do that?" he asked, jumping slightly in surprise.

"Do what?" she replied in a sweet, innocent voice.

"You know, like you know I'm there just before I get to you." His eyes narrowed suspiciously as he looked at her. She knew by his thoughts that he really did want to know, and not just about her knowing he was beside her.

Before she had come to live with Bill and Sally, Angelina had longed to be able to tell someone about her secret, but she had always been too scared. She had learned the hard way that people do not like people who are "different." Many times she had almost told Jordan, but she was still a little afraid.

"Have you finished the writing assignment for Miss Fisher yet?" she asked, trying to change the direction of his thoughts.

"Nah, it's a stupid assignment. Who really wants to write about what they want to do with the rest of their life? Gosh, I don't know what I want to do tomorrow, let alone the rest of my life." He grinned, not looking at her. *I do know what I want to do tonight!*

"So, write about what you want to do tonight." She waited as he caught his breath, wondering if she'd gone too far, and then turned to look at him.

"I, I can't! I mean, I don't know what I'm doing tonight, or, umm, what are you talking about?" Jordan had stopped walking and was now staring at her in a panic. Jason Morton, who wasn't watching where he was walking, plowed into Jordan, sending him and his books sprawling.

"Geez, Bradford, what are you doing stopping in the middle of the hall? Can't you see people are walking here?" Jason, taking large, exaggerated steps over and around Jordan and his books while laughing and jostling with his buddies, continued on down the hall. *He's such a loser.* Angelina stared at Jason's shoes. Suddenly he was laying flat on his face.

Scrambling to his feet, Jason punched the closest of his buddies, Travis Andrews. Trying to stop the flow of blood from his nose, he began to pick up his stuff, amid laughter and joking remarks.

"Hey, Morton, you got two left feet?" yelled Travis, rubbing his arm where Jason had just punched him.

"Say, Morton, you *trying* to copy Bradford?" Austin Thomas was laughing so hard he was snorting.

"OK, Morton, that was real cool. Now you're splashing your

blood everywhere. Yuk!" Amy Johnson turned away, looking as if she was about to faint.

Angelina grabbed Jordan's arm as all other thoughts were blocked from her mind. He seemed to be screaming inside her head; *"I hate Jason Morton. I hate Austin Thomas. I hate EVERYBODY! I wish I could just disappear."*

"I hope you don't hate me." Jordan raised his head slowly and turned to look into her smoky brown eyes, shock and wonder showing on his face. "Did I say that out loud? Wait a minute; did ***YOU*** say that out loud?"

As Angelina let go of Jordan's arm, her eyes clouded with anxiety and sudden fear. "Come on, we're going to be late for class."

Jordan stood for a second, watching her turn into Miss Fisher's writing class, then slowly following; he slipped into the seat next to her.

There IS something very different about her, he thought, *and I've got to find out just what it is.* He watched Angelina open her Creative Writing notebook and look toward Miss Fisher. He tried to concentrate on just her, not thinking about anything else. Nothing happened. *I wonder if I have to be touching her to hear her.* She seemed to tense up a little but did not turn to look at him. *I bet I do, but I don't think she has to be touching me to hear me. "Can you hear me, Angelina? Come on. Can ya hear me?"* Angelina continued to look at Miss Fisher.

Jordan sighed, shaking his head. *I must be losing my mind. What am I thinking; like she could really read minds, yeah right.*

Suddenly, Miss Fisher was asking Jordan a question. "So, Jordan, tell us what your paper is going to be about. What are you thinking of for a career?" The blank, dazed look on his face told her and the class his mind was a hundred miles away.

~ CHAPTER ONE ~

Angelina reached over with her foot and kicked Jordan's chair. He jerked with a start and slowly focused his eyes on hers. She nodded her head to the front of the class. Jordan turned toward Miss Fisher, who was standing with her arms folded, looking at him. "Um, what was the question again?"

The class broke out in wild laughter and hooting. Miss Fisher let it go for a few seconds and then quieted the students with a sharp rap of a ruler on her desk. Smiling, she repeated the question for him.

Jordan thought for a moment and then answered, "Well, I guess I haven't given an awful lot of thought lately to what I want to do with the rest of my life. I did want to be a pilot, but now, well, I'm not sure what I want to do. I have thought about working for the forest rangers, cause I could use a pilot's license with that line of work. Yeah, I think I just might like to pursue that kind of work." Jordan grinned at Angelina, proud of his quick recovery.

Miss Fisher smiled. "Well, I look forward to reading your paper on the subject." She paused for a moment, glancing at her notes, and then continued. "So, who else would like to share what...?"

Jordan did not hear the rest of Miss Fisher's question; all he heard was Travis loudly whispering to Jason and Austin. "Yeah, his old man used to be a pilot. Guess you could say he literally 'flew the coop'." He snorted at his own comment. Travis looked from Austin, who was shaking his head, to Jason who scowled and kicked his chair. "What?" Austin whispered, "I kinda feel sorry for his mom, ya know; no word, no nothin' all this time and suddenly gittin' slapped with divorce papers. What a jerk."

"Just shut up, both of you," Jason whispered hoarsely. Jordan's chair crashed to the floor from the force of him getting to his feet. His face turned red as he tightly clenched his fists. Miss

Fisher stopped talking and looked over in their direction.

"You shut up, Travis! You don't know anything about this," Jordan shouted, his eyes flashing in anger.

"Shove off, Bradford. Everyone knows you hate your old man," Jason answered, no longer trying to keep his voice low.

"And you love yours so much?" Jordan shot back at him. Jason was now on his feet, eyes blazing. Both boys stood facing each other, waiting for the other's next move.

Miss Fisher moved between them, her small frame taut with emotion. "Sit down, both of you. Do I need to send you to Principal Campbell's office?" She waited as both boys fought to control their anger. Glancing at Travis, she remarked, "And you, sir, will come back here as soon as you finish eating lunch. We're going to have a talk about respecting other people's privacy and appropriate things to say and not to say. Then, guess what, you get to write a paper on it."

The look of shock on Travis's face was almost worth the pain and embarrassment of the whole incident. Jordan felt himself starting to relax, but he kept his face blank. Miss Fisher turned back to face him. He tried to swallow the lump he felt in his throat as she continued in a tone that demanded his attention and respect. "I want you and Jason to see me tomorrow morning before school starts. I'll be waiting for you here. Understand?" She looked from Jordan to Jason. Both boys nodded without speaking. "Good." Turning, she walked back to her desk. Jason glared at Jordan and then turned back to his seat.

Jordan sat staring at the back of Jason's head. *Why is he such a jerk? He's always walking around with a chip on his shoulder. Doesn't he know how lucky he is to have both of his parents?* Jordan suddenly felt a hand on his arm. He turned to see Angelina looking at him. She smiled, pulling her hand back. "Are you OK?" she whispered.

Jordan nodded and opened his Creative Writing notebook and tried to concentrate on what Miss Fisher was saying. ". . . so your essay on what you want to do with your life will be due tomorrow. Your assignment for your term paper on Thursday is going to be an open assignment. You can write on any subject you like. When you turn in your paper tomorrow, or if you get done today, you can start working on the term paper." No one moved. "Well, go ahead, work on your papers."

Everyone started working. Jordan picked up his pen and sat staring at his paper. He chewed on his lip, thinking. He then made a short outline about what forest rangers did, specifically rangers who were also pilots. Then he began to write.

Angelina wrote quickly, detailing her own thoughts about being a veterinarian. She had always loved animals, all different kinds. She could read their feelings, and they could somehow understand her. She felt it was the perfect field for her because it would let her use her abilities without detection. Of course, she would not be able to put *that* in her paper. She shuddered, remembering Biology class in the ninth grade when they had dissected the frogs. She had felt the overwhelming sensation of fear and pain and had ended up getting a C- for refusing to dissect her frog. She only got the C- because Mr. Burns had let her look at Jordan's frog and write her report from it without doing the actual dissecting. She seemed to be doing better now with the whole idea of having to work on animals.

She glanced over at Jordan. He had kicked into gear. She smiled. He would make a good forest ranger, with the combination of his love for wild animals, nature, and flying. She watched as his hand, still honey brown tan in color, moved swiftly across the paper. She continued *listening* to his thoughts for a moment, and then returned to her own paper.

Angelina stared at her paper but found she could not keep her mind on the assignment. She gazed out the window at the big oak tree that was slowly dropping its leaves. Her mind drifted back in time, back to when she first came to live
with Bill and Sally Peters, her foster parents.

She smiled again, shaking her head; she remembered it like it was yesterday.

CHAPTER TWO

MEMORIES

Angelina knew she was in trouble with the first earsplitting scream. The clothes she had been floating through the air from her small worn suitcase to the open dresser drawer dropped in a heap to the floor. Anticipating at the very least a verbal attack, she turned cautiously to look up into the hysterical face of old Miss Applebee.

Miss Applebee looked so much like an apple it was almost comical. She was short, round, and her face was usually red. At the moment, though, it was very pale. Her grip on the doorknob was so tight her knuckles were white.

With a resigned sense of knowing, Angelina slowly got to her feet. Miss Applebee's mouth formed a round "O" as she sucked in air. Bringing her free arm up like a shield, her words came like violent missiles rocketing into the room. "NO! Don't move and don't speak. You are EVIL." She stumbled backwards and slammed the bedroom door shut, turning the key in the lock. The waddling stomp of her shoes on the hardwood floor seemed to make the walls shake. The frenzied dialing of the phone and the panic in her voice as she fairly screeched at Miss Simms, the county caseworker, filled Angelina with renewed despair.

"Miss Simms. Miss Simms! You best get back here right this minute. I will not have this evil girl in my house. Yes, right now." Her screeching voice cracked with her last words.

Angelina sighed. *Well, this is going to be the shortest stay yet. I wonder where they'll dump me this time.*

Angelina was not sure just when she had first realized she could do things other kids could not. As far back as her earliest memories, she could remember being able to do the things she could do, almost without thinking about it. Like standing in a crib with Teddy lying on the floor out of reach and *thinking* him to her, or seeing the cookies on the plate in the middle of the table and *thinking* one to her outstretched hand. She had discovered very early in life that most people did not take kindly to someone who was "different." She had become pretty good at hiding her secret, but after a while the temptation to show off would become too great. Once again she would find herself packing for yet another move.

She knew it was her own fault this time. Miss Applebee was hard to sense. Angelina had been thinking about how much she missed Felix, her last foster parents' pet cat, and so had been caught off guard. She slowly started repacking her things, trying to think how she was going to deal with the barrage of questions that were sure to come.

When Miss Simms arrived twenty minutes later, Angelina had decided to play dumb about the whole incident. This of course only fueled Miss Applebee's anger and her insistence that Angelina was an "evil" girl. In the end, Angelina carried her suitcase to the car and put it in the backseat. Kicking stones from the driveway into the street, she waited for Miss Simms, who was trying desperately to calm the still hysterical Miss Applebee.

Moments later, a frazzled Miss Simms was heading her beat-up station wagon north out of town. Surprisingly she was quiet, lost in her own thoughts. Angelina sat in the front seat, staring gloomily out the window. She knew they were leaving Appleton and going to a small town upstate, Baker's Bluff, about forty-five miles away. Angelina had lived her entire life, nine short years, in Appleton. After her mother had died in a car accident when she was five, she had lived in four different foster homes, not counting this last very short stay with Miss Applebee. Her thoughts drifted back in time to the last memory she had of being with her mother.

They had gone to the store to get a few groceries. Angelina was five years old but small for her age. She had begged her mother to let her ride in the cart. So her mother had picked her up and placed her in the seat of the shopping cart without too much difficulty. By simply putting her hands under her arms and making it look like she was picking her up, she was able to disguise the fact she was using telekinesis to *lift* her.

She remembered how tired her mother had been, slowly pushing the cart up and down the aisles, continually saying "no" to everything Angelina had asked for. She had pouted; folding her arms, refusing the hug her mother had tried to give her. She was too young to understand about not having enough money for potato chips but having enough for milk and bread and peas. As her mother walked away from the cart to select a few cans of soup, Angelina *thought* a bag of chips to the cart. Just before they reached the cart, her mother had turned to see them floating in the air. *"NO, Angelina, don't ever do that again."* Angelina still got goose bumps remembering the overwhelming fear she had felt from those unspoken words.

The fact that her mother had not spoken the words out loud was no surprise to her. They talked "without talking" to each other all the time. What she had been too young to realize then but fully understood now was the "NO" had not been said for her taking the chips when her mother had already said they could not afford them. The "NO" had been for *thinking* them to the cart, but her mother never had the chance to explain.

That was the day they had the car accident on the way home. Angelina could not remember exactly what happened. She did remember being startled by her mother's desperate thought, *"Oh, God, NO!"* Suddenly Angelina had been *lifted* through the open window of the car. She had flown through the air and landed gently on the ground off the side of the road just moments before the truck hit their car on the driver's side.

She remembered landing on her knees and turning to see the truck hit right where her mother was sitting. She could still hear the terrible crash, the shattering glass, the crunching of metal, and squealing tires as the car and truck slid locked together through the intersection, stopping only after slamming into the streetlamp pole. She remembered her mother's last heartbreaking thoughts to her. *"I'm sorry, Angelina. Take care of Teddy and always remember, I love you."*

Everyone who had seen the accident had sworn Angelina had been thrown from the car by the impact. What other explanation was there? It was a miracle she was unharmed. They had taken her mother away that day, under a white sheet. A kind and gentle policeman had held Angelina while she cried.

She had no memory of grandparents or a father either, so she had been placed in four different foster homes from the ages of five to nine. Each stay was just a littler shorter than the previous.

Whenever she would finally break down and show off, the other children would tell on her. They in turn would be punished for lying. After all, the things they claimed she could do were *not natural.* When they tried to make her do the *not natural* things to prove what they said, for some reason she could not do them. This, of course, did not endear her to them. She earned many bruises for her non-compliance along with spending much time behind locked closet doors.

Angelina rubbed her forehead in frustration. This last placement with Miss Applebee was the shortest yet, and she knew Miss Simms was becoming frustrated with her. She glanced sideways at her and could tell she was still brooding over the whole episode. Miss Simms was easy to sense, and her thoughts were so loud she might as well have been shouting them aloud.

I should have known better than to place Angelina with that Applebee woman. She's such a skittish, fussy old crab. Imagine trying to say Angelina can make things move without touching them. It's ridiculous. But where else could I have put her until the Peters decided if they were going to take her? And why is Angelina being so difficult? I wonder what really happened.

Miss Simms glanced at Angelina, who quickly turned to stare out the side window. She cleared her throat, and Angelina slowly turned back to look at her.

"The people I'm taking you to are a middle-age, childless couple. Their names are Bill and Sally Peters. They've wanted to foster a child for some time now. They're a little selective, though, on whom they are willing to take. They always ask to read the files on the different kids I offer them before they make a decision. So far, you're the only one they have agreed to take." She glanced at Angelina, who had turned toward the side window again. "Are you listening to me, Angelina? This is serious. I can't stress enough how important it is for you to not do anything to cause the Peters to question their decision to take you."

Miss Simms paused. Angelina continued to stare out the window. Finally Miss Simms sighed and said, "Well, if I get a call from them to come and get you, I will be forced to put you in the county home. Trust me, you don't want that. I sincerely hope you don't screw this up, because I really believe the Peters are good people."

Angelina refused to look at Miss Simms, quickly rubbing the tears off her cheeks. Why did her mother have to die and leave her all alone? Why was she different from everyone else? Why could she do all these *unnatural* yet amazing things? Was there no one else like her out there?

Miss Simms sighed again, shaking her head sadly. *I just don't understand it. She's such a bright, soft-spoken young girl, so mature for her age. She's pretty, healthy, friendly; well, OK maybe a little quiet, but honestly, any foster parent should be thrilled to get her. So why is it so hard to keep her placed? I just can't figure it out.*

An hour later Miss Simms pulled into the driveway of a big, white two-story colonial house. The quiet street was lined with huge oak trees, their large branches forming a canopy over the street. The front porch had a swing on it, with a big bay window facing the street. A cat was sitting on the window seat, lazily watching a bird on the feeder that hung from the ceiling of the porch. There was a two-car garage just a few feet from the back door. One of the trees in the backyard was so big the fence along the neighboring yard came up to the tree and stopped, then started up again on the other side. So the tree was actually in both yards, its limbs so huge and spacious they seemed to be begging for a tree house.

Angelina slowly got out of the car. Her mind was spinning as she tried to take it all in at once. She noticed a boy sitting on the railing of the porch at the neighboring house, the one that shared the tree. He was watching her intently. She stared back at him for a second as his thoughts burst into her mind.

Wow. Wonder who she is? I bet she's come to live with Bill and Sally. She looks like she hasn't had a good meal in a long time, and, gosh, would ya look at those clothes. His silent snorting sent prickles of indignation down her spine.

Suddenly, he lost his balance. He started to fall backward, frantically flaying his arms in the air like a dozing cat suddenly caught off guard. Just before he hit the porch, he seemed to float for a second before landing gently on his back. Quickly, he scrambled to his feet and turned around to look at Angelina. A look of frustration and shock replaced the cocky look that had been on his face. Angelina smiled sweetly at him before turning to follow Miss Simms onto the porch.

From the moment Angelina met Bill and Sally Peters, she knew there was something very special about them. Just what, she was not sure, but she liked them, and they seemed to like her too.

"I understand there have been some *unnatural* occurrences attributed to you, Angelina," Mr. Peters stated as he held her eyes with his questioning gaze. His tone was not accusing or harsh, just curious.

"Oh, I'm sure Angelina won't be any trouble for you!" Miss Simms rushed to reassure.

Sally was gazing thoughtfully at Angelina. "No, I'm sure we won't have any trouble at all." Her voice was soft and held a kind and calm caring tone. Angelina didn't realize there were tears on her cheeks as she nodded her head vigorously in agreement.

As Miss Simms prepared to leave, she paused to give

Angelina a hug and whispered, "Don't blow this, kid. I think this is where you're supposed to be." Then she winked and hurried out to her car and drove away, waving as she turned the corner.

Angelina stayed out on the porch long after Miss Simms' car had turned the corner. She was thinking about what she had said. *"I think this is where you're supposed to be."* She hoped so. More than anything she wanted it to be true. Bill and Sally seemed so nice. There was something about Sally that vaguely reminded her of her mother, something about her hazel eyes. She glanced next door to see if the boy was still on the porch. He was nowhere in sight. The screen door opened behind her and Sally came out onto the porch.

Angelina was startled. *Why didn't I sense her coming?* She tried to read her thoughts before turning around but came up against a wall. *Why can't I hear her thoughts?*

She turned to look into Sally's kind, smiling eyes. "Want to come back inside? I can show you around and we can get you settled in your room." She opened the door and held it for Angelina to walk in ahead of her.

Angelina smiled and, nodding her head, walked back into the house. When she had first come in with Miss Simms, she had been overwhelmed by its size. It was even bigger on the inside than it had looked from the outside. The front entryway had a long, curving wooden stairway to a second-floor landing. Angelina grinned, visualizing sliding down the smooth railing. To her left she noticed the formal dining room and wondered if it was used only for special occasions like Thanksgiving and Christmas. She could see there was a door off the dining room into the kitchen. The smell of freshly baked chocolate chip cookies made her stomach growl alarmingly. She sighed with disappointment when Sally did not head in that direction.

~ CHAPTER TWO ~

The plank flooring sang a creaking melody as Angelina silently followed Sally through a large arched opening into a formal living room. The enormity of the room dwarfed the large, very comfortable-looking overstuffed chairs of blue and green plaid. Angelina ran her hand across the soft fabric of the cushioned window seat. She glanced around, hoping to see the cat she had seen earlier. The floor to ceiling bookshelf on each side of the window facing the house next door was full of interesting-looking books. Angelina wondered in passing if she would be allowed to read any of them.

"There are lots of books here, so feel free to come down and get one anytime you want. The filing system I have is quite simple. The books are in order by the author's last name." Sally smiled as Angelina gave her a surprised look.

Another large arched opening led into what looked like a family room off the living room. A big fieldstone fireplace held the promise of cozy fires on cold winter evenings. A cool breeze ruffled the edges of the curtains framing the French doors that opened onto a large deck. Another corner was filled with the dark smoky gray screen of a big hushed television. Angelina ran her hand along the smooth surface of the large dapple-gray leather sofa, longing to sink into its deep cushions. The round table behind the couch held the promise of fun-filled evenings spent playing the board games that were stacked in the nearby cabinet.

Angelina slowly followed behind Sally, trying to take it all in, her eyes large with wonder. She dropped to her knees at the laundry room door to pet the cat, who Sally informed her was Alex. The bathroom was across the hall. The smell of lilacs came from a burning candle on the back of the toilet. Again, the smell of freshly baked cookies churned her insides as she and Sally passed the open doorway to the kitchen. She looked longingly back down the hallway as they ended at the front of the house.

Sally stopped, resting her hand on the railing of the staircase. "Are you ready to see the upstairs and where your room will be?"

"Yes, ma'am. You sure have a nice house. You must be awfully rich." Angelina suddenly felt the heat rise in her face and wished more than anything she could take back what she had just said. *What's wrong with me? Why did I say that?* She cautiously glanced at Sally, who was looking at her with a funny little smile on her face, eyes twinkling with amusement. Angelina closed her eyes and groaned inwardly, wishing she could sink through the floor.

She slowly followed Sally up the stairs. At the top they turned right and went into the room that looked out over the front porch. The side window gave her a view of the neighboring house where the boy had been on the porch. Angelina stopped just inside the door, catching her breath as she looked around the room. The walls were powder blue, with a strip of tiny flowered wallpaper around the top, flush with the ceiling. There was a full-size bed with a canopy of white eyelet lace. The long dresser's mirror reflected the powder-blue overstuffed chair in the opposite corner of the room. The oak desk and its matching straight-back chair complemented the white bookcase. The walk-in closet was almost as big as the private bathroom. *Is this MY ROOM?* She reeled with excitement as she turned to look at Sally, who was smiling. "Well, do you think you will be comfortable here?"

It was too much. Angelina burst into tears and ran from the room. She was down the stairs and out the front door almost before she realized it. She sat down on the top step and dropped her head on her arms and cried. She didn't hear the screen door open or Sally walk across the porch. She just suddenly felt Sally sitting there, next to her, with her arm around her shoulder.

Angelina blubbered into her arms as she cried, "I'm so sorry. You must think I'm such an ungrateful crybaby. It's just, the bedroom, it's like you knew what I liked. It's so perfect. I just can't believe it. It's all so wonderful, I'm afraid to believe it for fear I'll wake up and find myself back in the attic bedroom at the Johnsons', or worse yet, back with Miss Applebee. She was really creepy." Angelina started to wipe her nose on her sleeve but stopped when Sally handed her a Kleenex.

Sally looked at her thoughtfully. "I think we should go shopping this afternoon. If everything you own is in that one little suitcase, you are definitely going to need a few things or your closet is going to look ridiculously empty. What do you think? Shall we leave Bill and Jordan, our next-door neighbor, to work on the tree house they are just starting to build while you and I go shopping?"

Angelina smiled through her tears and nodded her head. Suddenly she thought of something. "Is the bathroom off my bedroom just for me?"

Sally burst out laughing. Standing up, she pulled Angelina to her feet and gave her a big hug. "Oh, Angelina, I'm so glad you've come to live with us!"

Angelina's first week with the Peters was one of the best but hardest weeks of her life. She was happier than she could ever remember being, except for when her mom was still alive. She wanted desperately not to do anything that would cause Bill and Sally to change their minds about keeping her.

She met Jordan the first evening after she and Sally returned from shopping. He had come out the kitchen door with Bill and helped carry in all her packages. Angelina was so excited she could hardly talk straight. She could not remember ever going shopping and getting brand-new clothes. The fact she now had more than one pair of shoes was simply amazing to her.

They had stopped on the way home and picked up a couple of pizzas. The four of them had sat around the kitchen table eating pizza, drinking pop, and laughing, just getting to know each other. Jordan was really nice, but he seemed to have some deep hurt inside him that he was trying to work through. Angelina thought maybe Bill was trying to help him.

That first week, Jordan and Bill worked on the tree house every afternoon after Bill got home from his Auto Body Shop, which he owned and ran with the help of his brother, Alan. Angelina started helping them build the tree house the second afternoon. She was excited. When the tree house was finished, they would be able to get to it from either yard.

Angelina found she could *hear* Jordan's thoughts easily, but for some reason, she could not *hear* Bill or Sally's thoughts. At first she thought maybe she was not going to be able to do her *special* things anymore. Except if that was true, why could she hear Jordan's thoughts?

But then, Saturday morning, the last day of her first week with the Peters, Alex got his tail caught in a mousetrap in the garage behind a big stack of boxes. Angelina almost fell down the stairs trying to get to him. It happened so fast she was not able to *lift* herself to stop her fall. But when she did not hit the floor hard and she turned to look into the anxious faces of Bill and Sally, she thought for a moment maybe *they* had kept her from falling. They also did not seem to be surprised she knew Alex was in need of assistance out in the garage.

As Angelina sat gently holding Alex, reassuring him he would be OK, Sally carefully washed the cut tail and applied a spray that would prevent infection. *"Hold still, Alex. She's almost done. It won't hurt for long. Would you like a treat when we're done?"* As Alex purred a positive yes, a small tin of cat treats drifted slowly across the room and came to rest gently on the table beside her. Panic started to close her throat. *Oh NO! Now I've ruined everything.*

Tears began to stream down her face as she turned to look at Sally. She never got the chance to try to form an explanation or apology. Sally was smiling at her, and for the first time since her mother's death, Angelina heard a kind, gentle voice speaking to her in her mind.

"You didn't ruin anything, Angelina dear, and I think it's about time you, Bill, and I had a long, serious talk."

Angelina looked from Sally to Bill, who was grinning at her with a twinkle in his eyes, and then back to Sally. Alex purred contentedly on her lap, as a smile spread across her face. She rubbed the tears from her cheeks.

So they talked. Boy did they ever talk!

She had been with the Peters for six years now, and she had learned how to not be "not natural" and still be herself, very carefully.

~

The ringing of the bell brought her back to the present. Jordan was stuffing his things into his backpack. "Come on. Let's go get some lunch; I'm starving."

CHAPTER THREE

A LUNCHROOM ENCOUNTER

Angelina's stomach growled hungrily as her eyes scanned the selections for lunch. The aroma of hot hamburgers and crispy chicken nuggets filled the air. She could not decide which one she wanted. "Take the hamburger. I don't think the chicken nuggets are completely dead yet." Jordan chuckled over his own remark. Angelina sighed and reached for the hamburger plate.

"What did you write about for Miss Fisher?" Jordan asked, catching a fry as it slid off the edge of his plate.

"I want to be a veterinarian," she said, reaching for a bowl of Jell-O with strawberries. "That's what I am writing about: where I would like to go to school and how I would like to someday have my own animal clinic."

Jordan reached for an apple, then changed his mind and grabbed the chocolate chip cookies.

"So, Jordan, are you going to write about becoming a forest ranger? That would really go right along with your plans for becoming a pilot. I think it's a great idea. Is it really what you want to do with your life, or were you just trying to get out of a jam by saying the first thing that came to your mind? We're going to be juniors next year, so you must have some idea of what you want to do." Angelina picked up a carton of chocolate milk and handed her lunch ticket to Mrs. Aims, the cashier.

Why is he so down on himself? Just because his dad split on him and his mom doesn't mean he's going to turn out that way.

Jordan took two chocolate milks and handed his lunch ticket to Mrs. Aims.

"Only one milk Jordan." She punched his ticket, but waited until he put one of the milks back before returning it to him.

Jordan grinned at Mrs. Aims as he shrugged and turned to follow Angelina. *What an old battleaxe.* Angelina turned and looked at Jordan. "What?" he asked.

"Don't be unkind, Jordan. That's not who you really are." Angelina found some seats where they could sit undisturbed at an empty table by the windows.

Jordan sat down across from her but didn't touch his food. He watched as she picked up her hamburger and took a bite. Still he didn't eat. Sighing, she put her hamburger down and tried to swallow her food. "OK, what's the matter?"

"Don't you already know?" he asked, trying to keep his mind blank.

"Are we playing a guessing game, Jordan? How can I know what's wrong if you don't tell me?" She took a sip of her milk, trying to calm herself. Had she gone too far this time?

"It's just you always seem to know what I'm thinking, or where I am, or what I'm feeling. How do you do that?" he asked while cramming several fries all at once into his mouth.

"Think about it, Jordan. How long have we known each other?

I've lived next door to you for six years now. We spend so much time together I sometimes think I know you and what you are thinking and feeling better than I know myself. It's no great mystery or secret." She took another bite of her hamburger.

"Yeah, well whatever. I still think it's something else and you're just not telling me, and that's not fair because I tell you everything!" He took a bite of his hamburger. As he reached for his milk to wash it down, an Algebra book landed on the table with a loud thud, sending the milk carton and both their lunch trays sliding across the table.

"Hey, Bradford, you left your stupid book in class. Miss Fisher asked me to give it to you." Jason looked around at his little group, snickering. "I told her I'd be happy to *give it* to ya."

Mrs. Aims had walked over to Mr. Tolin, the school cook, and was pointing in their direction. "You better back off, Jason," Travis warned. "You're gonna get detention again." He turned and quickly walked over to another table.

Jason turned, grinning, and waved at Mr. Tolin. "Hey, just doin' what Miss Fisher asked me to do," he said with a shrug. As he turned to walk over to join Travis and Austin, he gave Jordan's chair a shove. As their eyes met, Jordan said through clenched teeth, "Knock it off, Jason." Jason laughed and continued over to his little group.

Angelina's hands were clenched. Her eyes followed Jason's swaggering walk. Jordan reached across the table and rested his hand on hers. "Don't, Angelina," he whispered. She turned a look of surprise on her face. "Now who's acting like they *know something*?" Her hands relaxed and she smiled at him. "Let's try to finish eating so we won't be late for Mr. Allen's European History class. OK?" Pulling both their trays back in front of them, she took another bite of her hamburger. Jordan grinned and continued eating his fries.

~ CHAPTER THREE ~

Ten minutes later they slipped into their seats just before the bell rang. Mr. Allen was standing in front of his desk, arms folded across his broad chest. He waited patiently for the class to settle in their seats. They were always a little rowdy and excited right after lunch.

He cleared his throat. "OK, ladies and gentlemen, let's settle down. We have a lot to go over today. Midterms are this Friday, so let's get started."

Angelina watched as Jordan flipped his notebook open and sat ready to take notes. She smiled, thinking this was one class that he really enjoyed. She was sure that Mr. Allen had a lot to do with it. He was one of those teachers who knew how to capture your interest and attention. You were not afraid to express your opinion, and he never put down a student. Even when Jason Morton first tried to disrupt the class, he handled him like a pro. Jason did not smart off in class again after that; in fact, he was actually a very different person when he was in Mr. Allen's class.

Angelina knew Jason respected Mr. Allen, and when he was in his class he really wanted to be different. Too bad he could not be like that all the time. She actually liked him a little when he was in this class. Even though she could always hear Jason's thoughts whenever she wanted, she still could not figure out why he was always so angry. One thing she knew for sure, he was a ticking time bomb. When that bomb went off, she didn't want to be anywhere around it.

Mr. Allen began the review by handing out an outline of the areas that would be covered on the exam. Then he spent thirty minutes going over the outline and answering questions.

Angelina liked Mr. Allen. She never did anything "odd" in his class. She sometimes wondered what he would do if she did and what he would think of her if he knew the truth about her. She had tried several times to read his thoughts, but for some reason, she could never clearly hear them. She could get bits and pieces but never enough to really know what he was thinking.

She knew there were still several families in and around Baker's Bluff who were descendents from the original twenty-five families who had been living in the area back in 1882. Maybe Mr. Allen was a descendent of one of those families. If he was, did that mean that he could do some of the things that she, Bill, Sally, and Uncle Alan could do? Were there others out there like them? If so, why didn't they communicate with each other more? Bill and Sally kept stressing how important it was not to let anyone know what she could do. If there really were others like them, wouldn't it be good to have a kind of support network in place to help each other?

She understood that some really terrible things had happened back then, but surely now they could keep those kinds of things from happening again. The benefits seemed to outweigh the danger. *Maybe sometime I'll tell him,* she thought. But she knew she wouldn't, not with out talking it over with Bill and Sally first. She just could not take the chance of ruining everything if Mr. Allen was not like them.

The ringing of the bell and Mr. Allen's voice saying they would continue to review the next day brought Angelina back to class. She sighed as she slowly stood up, reaching for her notebook. *Now I'll have to get Jordan to let me look over his notes again.*

"Ya been daydreaming, again?" Jordan asked as he closed his notebook on three full pages of notes. His voice held a gentle note of teasing.

She grinned at him. "Why should I take notes when you are so good at it and you always let me copy yours?" She laughed as he rolled his eyes at her and started for the door. "See ya after PE." he said. "You going to the library, or coming to watch us practice for Friday's game?"

"Practice, see ya." Angelina headed for the girls' PE door. They were in the pool today and were going to be tested for treading water, floating, and four different swim strokes. She wondered how Amy would do today. She was so afraid of the water. She always tensed up and seemed to fight the water instead of letting it carry her. Well, at least there was never a dull moment in this class!

CHAPTER FOUR

AN INCIDENT IN THE POOL

Mrs. Timson, the athletic coach for the girls, gave two sharp blows on her whistle. She had fifteen tenth-grade girls, and only three days to test them all, since Thursday and Friday were short days for midterms. She would only have them for today's class period and Wednesday, and then on Friday, so she really needed to start today to get them all tested by the end of class on Friday. Her eyes searched the sea of faces for her one problem student, Amy Johnson.

Amy was the only child of Dr. Anthony and Jill Johnson. They both worked at Baker's Bluff General Hospital, a twenty-bed facility with one surgery, small, but sufficient for the community.

She spotted her down at the far shallow end of the pool. She sighed, rubbing the ache in the back of her neck. Her head throbbed with the same old question, should she have her go first and get it over with or wait till last to put off the bad scene for as long as possible?

"All right, ladies, you know what we have to accomplish by

the end of class on Friday. I need four spotters." Mrs. Timson searched the faces of the girls who raised their hands to offer assistance. "OK, let's see . . . all right, Katie, I want you down at the shallow end. Melissa, I want you halfway to the middle with Abby halfway to the deep end. Angelina, I want you down here at the deep end with me. OK, ladies, here's the drill. You are going to swim one length of the pool, demonstrating four different types of strokes, floating, and treading water; any questions?"

"Are we going to be timed?" "Can we dive in and swim part way under water and have that count as a type of stroke?" "Do we ***have*** to dive in?" *Did I say anything about diving?* "Does floating on our back count as a type of stroke?"

Mrs. Timson closed her eyes and shook her head, sighing. Opening her eyes she looked at her clipboard; brows furrowed, and then blew on her whistle. Angelina watched as Mrs. Timson again glanced down at Amy who had not moved from where she sat. Mrs. Timson's frustrated thoughts sent tiny prickles of apprehension down Angelina's spine. *I just know she's going to be sick or faint or something. Well, I might as well get it over with.*

"OK, let's start with you, Amy. Come up to this end and you can dive in or jump in, whatever you want." Mrs. Timson turned her back to Amy so she did not have to see the fear in her eyes and walked to the other side of the pool.

Amy got up slowly and walked to the deep end. Her face had lost all color. *Oh, I can't do this! She knows I'm scared. Why is she making me go first?* Angelina, sensing her panic and dread, moved to the deep end and waited. As Amy walked to the edge of the pool and tried to calm her breathing, she sent one last imploring look at Mrs. Timson, who only nodded at her to begin.

Angelina tried to catch Amy's eye to give her a reassuring

look, but Amy was not seeing anything, she was only feeling dread. Tensing up, she leaned forward, bent her knees and pushed off the side of the pool.

She hit the water with a hard smack and immediately started to sink. Mrs. Timson sighed, shaking her head and looked at Angelina. Angelina paused only long enough to try and read Amy's mind but came back with nothing. Her body cut the water with a perfect dive, hardly causing a ripple. Upon reaching Amy she extended the shield around herself to include Amy. Coming up behind her, she slipped her arm around Amy's waist and jerked hard, causing Amy to spit out the water she had already swallowed. Suddenly Amy's eyes were open and she started to fight Angelina. *"Relax, Amy, I've got you. You're going to be all right."* Amy's head turned to look at Angelina, her eyes round with shock, and then she passed out. *Well, maybe this is better; maybe she won't remember anything.* Just before they cleared the surface of the water, Angelina released her shield.

"She's unconscious," she yelled, spitting water. "Somebody give me a hand." Abby, who had been closest to Angelina, had jumped into the water once she could see that she had Amy. She swam over to Angelina to try to help her with Amy. Melissa was kneeling at the side of the pool reaching for Amy, and Katie had run to get the giant hook from the wall. Other girls now moved forward to try to help.

Mrs. Timson pushed through the crowding girls. "Step back, ladies, we need some room here to work."

They got Amy out of the pool and laid her gently down on the cement a foot from the edge of the pool. Melissa looked up at Mrs. Timson, the anxiety in her voice reflecting the concern in her eyes. "She's breathing, but I can't get her to wake up."

~ CHAPTER FOUR ~

Mrs. Timson looked questioningly at Angelina. "She couldn't have hit her head, could she? I mean, it didn't look like she went in that deep."

Angelina had pulled herself out of the water and was now kneeling beside Amy. She did not look up or answer Mrs. Timson as she gently felt Amy's head for any lumps without moving her neck. Amy was breathing, and Angelina could feel a strong pulse in her neck. "No, I think she's just suffered a shock. She should come around any minute." Looking up at Mrs. Timson, she continued, "Maybe someone should go and get Miss Briemont? Maybe we should get Mr. Campbell too."

Mrs. Timson looked slightly annoyed and worried all at the same time. "Yes. Yes, I guess that would probably be a good idea. Katie? Oh, there you are. Go get them both. The rest of you, get back so we have room to work on her." There was a slight undercurrent of shaky voices and the beginnings of hysteria from the crowding girls. "All right ladies, calm down. She's going to be OK. Could one of you girls bring a couple of towels over here so we can cover her up a little, to keep her from getting chilled?"

Melissa took the outstretched towels and covered Amy, putting a folded one carefully under her head. Her eyes met Angelina's and she bit her lip to stop the trembling. Abby held one of Amy's hands, gently rubbing it. "Hey, Amy, come on, wake up! You're not getting off testing this easy." She looked up at Angelina, a tear slipping down her cheek.

Angelina took a deep breath, focusing on Amy's face. She reached out and touched Amy's leg. *"Be careful Angelina. Don't be too obvious with what you're doing."* Angelina jerked her hand back and glanced around. *"Sally? Where are you?"*

"I'm in the car. I'm almost to the school. I'm going to tell

Mr. Campbell I was coming by to give him an update on the progress of the plans for the homecoming dance. I should be there in less than three minutes."

"Should I wait?" Angelina chewed her lip.

"Yes. I'm pulling up right now."

Moments later Miss Briemont, the school nurse, came through the doors at the far end of the pool, closely followed by a white-faced Katie. Mr. Campbell stopped in the doorway and turned to look at who was calling out to him in the hall.

"Let me through, girls, let me through." Miss Briemont hurried through the now parting crowd of girls, and reached Amy just as Angelina slipped some folded towels under Amy's lower legs to elevate them to prevent shock. "Thank you, Angelina. OK, let's take a look here."

As Miss Briemont slowly examined Amy, Mr. Campbell came walking up, talking to Sally. Mrs. Timson walked over to him and began to fill him in on what happened. Angelina caught Sally's eye. *"I don't know if I should have shielded her. She came to under the water, but there wasn't any water, and I think that's what put her into shock. I'm scared, Sally: I really screwed up this time. I'm really sorry."*

Sally walked over and knelt down beside Miss Briemont. "Anything I can do to help, Ann?" she asked, reaching out her hand and gently touching Amy's leg. Very discreetly she focused her eyes on Amy's face.

"I'll tell you in a minute, once I've finished examining her. I can't understand why she is still unconscious." Miss Briemont leaned over to check Amy's pupils.

"She will not remember anything after hitting the water." Angelina looked from Sally to Amy, as Amy suddenly started to stir.

~ CHAPTER FOUR ~

"Take it easy, Amy," Miss Briemont said, helping her to sit up slowly. Amy looked around and then turned to look at Angelina.

"What happened?"

With only twenty minutes left of class, Mrs. Timson told the girls they could practice their strokes or go into the locker room to change for their next class.

Sally was waiting for Angelina when she came out of the girls' locker room. Angelina looked at her, nervously running her fingers through her still damp hair, causing the strong smell of chlorine to precede her. "How did you know what happened?"

Sally smiled. "You were broadcasting so loud that both Bill and Alan contacted me. I convinced them that if we all three showed up it would look a little suspicious."

Angelina sighed. "I guess I just didn't think. I was so worried about her inhaling too much water. I also just discovered today that anyone can hear my thoughts if I make physical contact at the same time." Angelina glanced around to see if anyone was listening. "Something happened today in the hall, and Jordan got really mad. I reached out and grabbed his arm and thought something, and I know he heard it."

Sally stopped walking and looked at Angelina. "Well, I'm glad that Amy is going to be alright. I guess it was just the shock of it all that made her lose consciousness. Oh, hi, Jordan! How's your mom coming along with her book?"

Jordan came walking up to them, his eyes dancing with excitement. "Wow, you had an exciting swim class, Angelina! It's already all over school how Amy almost drowned and you single-handedly saved her. Oh, hi, Mrs. Peters; ah, my mom? Ah, her book? Oh, she's almost finished with it. No thanks to my jerk dad!" Jordan scowled and kicked the locker.

Sally smiled at him, "Oh, come on, Jordan. Give your mom some credit. I think she's going to be a great writer! She's actually dealing with things a lot better than you know." Sally turned to Angelina. "Well, I guess I better go and find Mr. Campbell so I can finish my talk with him about the homecoming dance. See you tonight, Angelina."

Sally turned and headed for the office. Glancing back, she waved at them both. "Tell your mom I said come over tomorrow and we can catch up on each other's news." Jordan stood there staring at her as she disappeared around the corner.

Slowly he turned toward Angelina and smiled as they headed down the hall toward their last class period, study hall. "So? Are you going to tell me what really happened or not?"

CHAPTER FIVE

THE ARGUMENT

Angelina continued walking down the hall, trying not to let Jordan see how nervous he was making her with his questions. "What do you mean what 'really' happened? She dove in and did a giant belly smacker and knocked herself out. I jumped in and pulled her to the edge of the pool and she came to after a few minutes. No big deal." Angelina tried to make her voice sound casual and yet convincing as she nervously ran her fingers through her still damp hair.

"Yeah, whatever; everyone is saying that when you were both underwater it looked like you were in some kind of a bubble or something. What's that all about?" Jordan followed her into study hall. Sitting down, he folded his arms on top of his books and stared at her.

Angelina sighed and opened her Algebra book to work on the problems Mr. Crawford had said would be due the following day. "I have no idea what you or they are talking about," she whispered, glancing up to see if Mr. Tolin was looking in their direction. "Things always look strange through the water, you know that. Water distorts things. Have you been paying attention at all to anything in our Physical Science classes?"

She knew her voice sounded harsh and a little tense, but she was not prepared for the look in Jordan's eyes or for the confusion and hurt in his thoughts.

Why is she snapping my head off? I wonder what really happened and why she's trying to hide it from me. I thought she trusted me. Jordan tried to keep the hurt and disappointment from his face. Suddenly his eyebrows shot up. *"If you can read my thoughts like I think you can, why don't you trust me? Come on, Angelina, why won't you tell me what's really going on?"*

Angelina couldn't stop herself. Her mouth fell open and she just stared at Jordan. "I knew it!" he whispered fiercely, reaching out to steady her shaking hand, "You can hear my thoughts, can't you?"

She quickly pulled her hand away from him and looked up at Mr. Tolin, who was now frowning at them and shaking his head. *"Sally!"* She grabbed her book to try and steady her hands. *"Sally. Help me. I'm scared."*

"Angelina, calm down, honey. You need to try and relax. Don't react to what he's saying. He doesn't know anything for sure." Angelina swallowed hard. Then she narrowed her eyes and made her face reflect suspicion. "I wonder if this will have any effect on our plans for the homecoming dance."

A look of confusion passed across Jordan's face. "What?"

Angelina glanced over at Mr. Tolin, who was helping another student with a History question. She leaned forward and whispered, conspiratorially, "Yeah, when you asked about what happened it reminded me that Sally was coming in today to talk to Mr. Campbell about the homecoming dance, and well, I just hope that after this stupid episode with Amy he'll still let us do what we want for the dance. Why? What did you think I was getting all shook up about?" She flipped her long, mousy-brown hair over her shoulder and picked up her pencil.

Jordan shook his head, as if trying to clear the cobwebs of confusion away. As he studied her face, his eyes narrowed with suspicion, but he did not answer her. Angelina forced herself to not look away but continued to meet his gaze eye to eye, maintaining a look of waiting for his answer. Jordan finally looked down, grabbed his pencil, and opened his Algebra book. "Just forget it!" he muttered under his breath and started working on the problems.

Angelina's face clouded over as she watched him start working the problems. She fought to keep her tears from coming. *"I wish I could be honest with him! I don't think it would matter to him."*

"Not just yet, Angelina. Trust me." Sally's silent words held no comfort.

Angelina looked down at the problems and tried to concentrate on the work she had in front of her. *"OK, Sally, but it's not easy keeping secrets from your best friends. I think both Jordan and Abby are beginning to suspect things. Wouldn't it be better to tell them the truth than to let them continue imagining all those wild things they are thinking about me? The truth isn't nearly as scary as what they've been thinking!"*

"I'm not worried about how they will take the truth - it's what they will do with it that has me concerned."

Angelina tried to work on the Algebra problems, but she could not concentrate. She kept going over in her head all the reasons she felt justified in telling Jordan about her abilities. Every now and then his frustrated thoughts over the Algebra problems would burst into her consciousness, and she would glance at him out of the corner of her eye. They always did their Algebra together, since she seemed to understand it better and would help him work through the problems. Now, because he was mad at her, he was refusing to even look at her.

She could understand Sally's hesitation with Abby. Her dad was the minister of Baker's Bluff Bible Church. They would immediately think of witchcraft and all that "New-Age" stuff. But Jordan, well Jordan was different.

She thought back to some of the things Bill had told her one evening a couple of years ago when she had wanted so badly to share her secret with Abby. He had told her then about the meteor that fell in 1882. How after just a few short years many of the people discovered that they had developed unique abilities. Not everyone developed the abilities, and slowly an atmosphere of fear, suspicion, and mistrust began to grow in the little settlement, to the point that even those who shared in the abilities began to withdraw from each other.

It still did not make any sense to her. They should have stuck together. Instead, one tragedy after another had happened: barns mysteriously catching on fire, mining accidents that should never have happened, a bull somehow getting loose, resulting in the awful death of a little four-year-old girl. Still, she could not help but wonder if there were others who had these same extraordinary abilities still living in Baker's Bluff. Maybe one of them would know who her mother had been. She must have lived around here somewhere. That must be why she could do all the things she could do. It was all such a mystery -- one she desperately wanted to solve.

The ringing bell startled Angelina back to her surroundings. Jordan slammed his book shut, pushed his chair back, and stood up.

~ CHAPTER FIVE ~

He stuffed his Algebra book and notebook into his backpack, and without a word, turned and walked out of the study hall and headed for football practice.

Abby slipped into the seat next to Angelina. "You two have a fight?"

Angelina sighed and dropped her head on her open book. *Great! One leaves off and the other steps in to take over!*

CHAPTER SIX

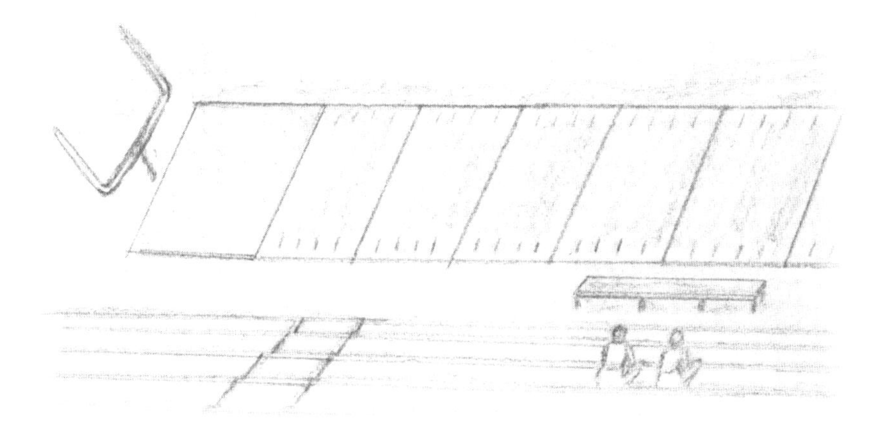

THE ATTACK

Angelina waited at Abby's locker as she packed her books in her backpack. "Are you going to go watch the guys practice?" she asked, almost shouting over the mixture of noises filling the crowded hall.

Before Abby could respond, Marney Burns came rushing up, pushing her glasses up on her nose. Papers were haphazardly sticking out of her backpack as if she had hurriedly stuffed them in before leaving her Spanish class. "Wow! Like cool! PE was so awesome! What you did was soooooo cool, Angelina. I was scared to death! I just knew Amy was going to drown or something worse. She hardly swallowed any water. You two looked so funny underwater, and if it hadn't been so scary, I probably would have laughed."

Abby looked at Angelina and grinned, rolling her eyes. Angelina winked back. With Marney, you did not really need to answer. It was almost like she did not expect an answer; she just kept rattling on and on. Angelina had said before she was sure it was due to the fact that Marney was just too smart and her brain and mouth were in constant competition with each other.

The girls all walked together down the hall toward Angelina's locker, only half listening to Marney's nonstop dialog. Once they reached Angelina's locker, Marney said good-bye and continued her chatter with the next person she ran into. Abby shook her head, laughing, while Angelina packed her backpack. "So, are you going to watch the guys practice or head for the library?" Angelina shut her locker, waiting for Abby's response.

"Watch the guys, of course!" Both girls laughed as they headed out the door for the football field.

A cool breeze ruffled Angelina's hair as she and Abby sat down on the metal bleachers and prepared to watch the guys practice. The strong scent of burning leaves filled the air. Angelina breathed in deeply as she reached for her backpack to pull out her writing notebook. She stopped suddenly when Abby asked, "So, what *were* you and Jordan arguing about?"

Angelina sighed and tried to steady her voice. "Oh, it's the same old thing. He thinks I'm keeping secrets from him." She paused as she struggled with the mounting tension and frustration that was rising inside her. "He's becoming obsessed about it. I really don't know what to do to make him understand I DON'T HAVE ANY SECRETS!"

Abby pulled back a little and raised her eyebrows, while several girls who had just sat down not far from them all turned to stare.

"Sorry," Angelina said, blushing. "It's just that he's driving me crazy with this stupid idea that I'm keeping secrets from him."

Abby was silent for a minute, nervously picking at a string hanging from her backpack. "Well, aren't you?" she asked, cautiously glancing at Angelina's troubled face.

Angelina stared at Abby. Abby was her best friend, her "almost sister." She had wanted to tell Abby, almost more than Jordan, about her strange abilities. But Abby was a preacher's kid; what would she think? Wouldn't she feel like she had to tell her parents? Angelina did not think Abby really believed that she was a witch, nor was she worried about the "New-Age" stuff. Would she be able to keep the secret? Abby was so close to her parents; wouldn't she feel obligated to tell them? What would *they* think? What if she told and everyone got scared of her; would she and Bill and Sally have to move?

Sudden gasps and screams, coming from the other girls on the bleachers, and a commotion on the field, interrupted her brooding.

Down on the field there was mass confusion as Greg Burns and some of his friends tried to keep Travis Andrews and Austin Thomas away from Jordan who was lying, unmoving, on the ground. Mr. Timson had already pushed Jason Morton out of his way as he knelt down to check on Jordan. Jill Morton, the cheerleading captain and Jason's older sister, had started to run out on the field with Mrs. Timson but stopped dead still when Mr. Timson yelled to his wife to call 911.

Angelina was down on the field and running toward Jordan almost before she realized she had moved. *"NO! NO! JORDAN!!! OH, GOD, NO! SALLY, HELP. JORDAN'S BEEN HURT."*

"I know, Angelina," Sally's strong, calm thoughts came instantly into Angelina's frantic mind. *"An ambulance is on the way. Don't let them move Jordan at all. Bill is almost there. Just pray, Angelina honey."*

Tears were streaming down Angelina's face as she dropped

to the ground beside Jordan and Mr. Timson. "Don't touch him or move him at all," she gasped through her sobs. She reached out and touched his arm.

"Jordan? Oh, Jordan! Can you hear me? Jordan, please, you have to be all right. Please! I can't lose you!"

With Angelina now kneeling beside Jordan, Mr. Timson jumped up and rounded on Jason, shouting his anger and frustration. "What were you thinking? Get off this field! Don't talk to me. Get out of my face. You better wipe that smirk off your face too, mister. In fact, I'm suspending you from this Friday's game and maybe from the last three games as well. Don't say anything to me right now. Just get out of my sight." Mr. Timson turned back to Jordan but suddenly went sprawling on the ground as Jason lunged at him, pushing him to the ground.

Mr. Campbell, who was running across the field, with Miss Briemont, Mr. Damon, the band teacher, and Bill Peters, was yelling at Jason Morton. Greg Burns tackled Jason from behind as he was getting ready to kick Mr. Timson. Greg sat on him until Mr. Campbell reached them.

"WHAT IS GOING ON HERE!" thundered Mr. Campbell.

Everyone started talking at once. Mr. Campbell began firing questions at different students as Bill Peters knelt down by Jordan.

"Try to distract Miss Briemont a minute, Angelina."

"OK." Angelina stood up and fell into Miss Briemont's arms, sobbing. Miss Briemont struggled to keep herself and Angelina from falling. Bill carefully ran the flat of his hand under Jordan's head and neck and body, slightly levitating his entire body not more than an inch from the ground and then gently lowering him before anyone noticed what he was doing. *"He's got a concussion, a dislocated shoulder, and maybe a ruptured spleen; I can't be sure. I do know we*

need to get him to the hospital as soon as possible."

Bill caught Angelina's eye and saw the panic she was feeling. *"Steady little girl."* They both turned to look downfield when they heard the crying siren of the approaching ambulance. Michael Reed pulled the ambulance onto the football field and almost before it stopped, he and his partner, Joel Bolton, jumped from the vehicle.

"Get back!" Mr. Campbell thundered at the students who had now congregated on the field. Mr. Campbell and two other teachers grabbed hold of Jason and started walking him over to the police car that was just pulling up with Police Chief James Waits in it.

As the squad door swung open and Chief Waits stepped out, he asked, "What's going on here, Alex?"

"Well, apparently Jason here, and his cronies, decided to beat the heck out of Jordan Bradford. I'm not sure how seriously he's hurt. I will not tolerate this kind of behavior!" Mr. Campbell was frowning at Jason.

"Have you got anything to say, Jason?" questioned Chief Waits.

"Yeah, I do!" Jason shouted angrily, jerking his arms free from the hold that Mr. Campbell and Mr. Timson had on him. He glared angrily at each man in turn as he continued. "You just wait till my old man gets here. You'll be sorry you messed with me. You can't pull *me* from the game. This team is *nothing* without *me*!" Jason's hands were balled into fists, and he was shaking with pent-up rage.

Suddenly Jill stepped in front of him. Her eyes flashed with anger at her brother. Raising her hand, she slapped him hard across the face. Jason's hand flew to his face, his eyes registering shock. "Grow up, Jason!" she hissed. "You better pray Jordan's not seriously hurt. And about Dad, well, *you're* the one who's gonna be sorry." Jill turned to walk over to Angelina but paused to look into

Mr. Campbell's surprised face and then turned back to Jason. "Oh, and about the team -- I believe the general consensus is that the team would probably be better off *without you* if you continue to act like a child. My advice to you is: if you want to stay on the team, you better get a grip on your anger and pride. If you don't, well, you're heading for a hard fall."

Jill turned back to Angelina and was rewarded with a smile, which she returned in spite of her quivering lips. Just as she reached for Angelina's hand, she saw Mr. Allen step from behind Mr. Campbell. As their eyes met, she saw a kind look of pride in his eyes, and he nodded slightly at her.

Mr. Allen put his hand on Mr. Campbell's shoulder and started to speak but was interrupted when Michael Reed stepped forward. "We're taking Jordan to the hospital. I've already called them and they are contacting his mother. Dr. Johnson is at the ER waiting for us now. At the very least Jordan probably has a concussion and a dislocated shoulder. He may also have a ruptured spleen; so the sooner we get him there the better. I'll keep you posted, Chief Waits." Then Michael turned back to Jordan and helped Joel load the gurney into the ambulance.

Angelina hurried back to the bleachers for her backpack and then ran to catch up with Bill since they were going to follow the ambulance to the hospital. They both knew that Sally had gone next door so she could be with Evelyn, Jordan's mom when the hospital called her, and was going to drive her in Evelyn's car to the hospital.

Mr. Allen stood looking at Jason, who was still holding his face and was now looking scared and ashamed. Turning to the principal and the police chief, he said in a low voice that made Jason's hands shake, "Alex, James, I think that Jason, Travis, and Austin should all be put on probation." He paused to glance at Jason, who had now lost all color in his face. "I'm thinking four weeks of detention with me should do the trick. What do you think?"

Mr. Timson looked at Mr. Campbell and was pleased to see a calm smile spread across his face. "Yes, George," Mr. Campbell said in a quiet firm voice, "I think that is an excellent idea."

Angelina sat quietly crying in the car as Bill drove to the hospital. He tried once to reassure her that Jordan was going to be all right, but she could not stop crying and she just did not feel like talking. Her thoughts and feelings were in such a jumble, she could hardly think straight.

This is entirely my fault. If I hadn't made Jason trip and fall in the hall this morning after he knocked Jordan down, maybe he would not have been so mad at Jordan. If only I'd been watching instead of talking to Abby, maybe I could have prevented the whole thing. He has to be OK. I can't imagine what it would be like if Jordan weren't here.

Bill reached over and patted her arm just as Sally spoke to both of them. *"We're at the hospital. Dr. Johnson is examining Jordan right now. Angelina, this is not your fault. I'm sure Jordan is going to be all right. Dr. Johnson says he should regain consciousness real soon, and he's sure he doesn't have a ruptured spleen. The doctor is going to put his shoulder back in while he's still unconscious. I'll see you both when you get here."*

Angelina took the hankie that Bill held out to her and wiped the tears off her face. He smiled at her. "It's going to be OK, kiddo, and Sally's right. This is not your fault. Jason's been a powder keg waiting to go off for a long time. It was bound to happen. Now we just have to deal with it and see what we can do to help." Angelina nodded silently, and turned to stare out the window.

CHAPTER SEVEN

JORDAN AGREES TO HELP

Angelina sat in the chair next to Jordan's bed, holding his hand. The crisp white sheets beneath her hands were cool to the touch and smelled strongly of bleach. Jordan was still unconscious. Thankfully, he did not have a ruptured spleen, but he did have a concussion, and Dr. Johnson had put his dislocated shoulder back in and said he should regain consciousness soon. Sally and Evelyn talked softly at the other end of the room. Bill went to the hospital office to wait for Mr. Campbell, as they were going to make arrangements for the school to foot the entire bill for the emergency room and the overnight stay.

Angelina felt a lump forming in her throat as she looked at Jordan. The left side of his face was bruised and puffy and his eye was already turning black. Still, even unconscious, he looked sweet and peaceful. She closed her eyes, as her thoughts pounded in her already throbbing head like a sledgehammer on rock.

He must have still been upset from our talk in study hall.

That's probably why Jason was able to get him on the ground. Please, God, he has to be all right. What would I do if something happened to him? He's very important to me, God, and I've never even told him how I feel. I guess I've kind of taken him for granted, thinking he would always be there. Please make him be OK. I think Sally is wrong too to worry about Jordan at least. He wouldn't do anything to hurt me or get me in trouble. I wish I'd have told him a long time ago. Please, God . . Angelina's head jerked up and her eyes flew open as Jordan squeezed her hand; she looked deeply into his smiling brown eyes.

"You can hear my thoughts, can't you? I can hear yours when you touch me!"

Angelina turned to look at Sally, who was looking at them. Evelyn hurried to the other side of the bed.

"Jordan!" Her voice broke with a sob, and she took his hands. Jordan turned his head to look at her and said, "I'm OK, Mom; please don't cry."

Angelina stood up and walked over to Sally. *"I'm sorry, Sally, I didn't know he was awake."*

"Don't worry about it. I'm sure everything will be all right." "Evelyn, Angelina and I are going to step outside and leave you and Jordan alone for a few minutes. Can I get you some coffee or water or something?"

Evelyn was wiping her eyes with a tissue and nodded at them. "Coffee, please, and thanks."

Walking down the hospital hallway, Angelina could not bring herself to look at Sally. Instead, she focused on the floor, the square and diamond shaped tiles forming a flowing pattern. *"Angelina, don't worry. It's going to be all right. Jordan is going to be just fine, and if he has figured out that you can hear his thoughts, well, we'll just have to hope that he cares enough for you to keep your secret."* Sally stopped outside the door to the small guest and staff cafeteria and touched Angelina on the arm. *"I am going to ask that you not talk about it with Abby just yet. I still haven't got a clear feeling about her. OK?"*

Angelina looked at Sally, pain and fear in her eyes. *"OK, Sally, I'll do whatever you and Bill ask me to do. You two are my family now. I feel safe with you, and I don't want anything to happen to put any of us in danger. Why do people have to be afraid of what they do not understand?"*

Sally grinned as she pushed the door open. *"Honey, if I had the answer to that question, I could probably make enough money so none of us would ever have to work again."*

Angelina grinned back and started to relax for the first time that day. What a long day it had been. Way too much had happened. Well, at least Jordan wouldn't be going to Baker's Books & Stuff and getting into trouble trying to shoplift the Flight Masters' video game.

"Pick out something you think Mrs. Bradford would eat and something for yourself too. We'll take it back to the room and visit for a little longer, then head for home." Sally reached for a salad and roll, and then walked toward the checkout.

Angelina picked out a tuna sandwich and a couple oatmeal cookies for herself and Mrs. Bradford and walked over to the register. Sally had two coffees and a carton of chocolate milk sitting at the side of the register.

Walking back to the room, Angelina began to feel nervous again. *"Honey, he's not going to say anything to you "out loud" in front of his mother. I feel certain of that. Don't worry; everything is going to be all right. I promise."*

Angelina smiled at Sally before walking into Jordan's room.

Jordan looked up at her and grinned. Mrs. Bradford smiled and motioned Sally toward the two chairs she had pulled up closer to the bed. Angelina handed her a tuna sandwich and a cookie and then walked so she could sit at the head of the bed. Sally handed the chocolate milk to her, then turned to Mrs. Bradford and began talking softly to her, encouraging her to try to eat some of the food they had brought.

Jordan smiled at Angelina, winked, and then said, "So, what happened to Jason? Did he get expelled? I wasn't expecting to be tripped from behind, and once I was down, wow, he sure lit into me."

Angelina began to unwrap the cellophane from around her tuna sandwich, her hands trembling in frustration. "I'm not really sure what happened to him, Jordan. When we left, Chief Waits was still talking to Mr. Timson and Mr. Campbell. Mr. Allen had just walked up. I think at the very least Jason should be expelled."

She took a bite of her sandwich and tried to steady her shaking hands. Jordan watched her quietly, waiting for her to continue. She swallowed and took a sip of her chocolate milk before continuing. "I didn't see you get tripped. I was talking to Abby when the girls farther over on the bleachers began to scream. When I saw you, Mr. Timson had already pushed Jason aside and was checking to see how badly you were hurt." Tears began to stream down Angelina's face, and she tried to turn away. Jordan reached out and caught hold of her hand. *"Don't cry, Angelina, I'm OK. It's gonna be all right. I'm NEVER going to leave you or do anything to put you in harm's way. Do you trust me?"*

Angelina glanced over at Sally who was listening to Mrs. Bradford relate again what the doctor had told her after he had worked on Jordan. Sally gave her a slight nod. Angelina turned back to Jordan and looked him in the eye.

~ CHAPTER SEVEN ~

"Trust you? TRUST YOU? Why, only with my life -- only with all my heart!" Jordan gripped her hand tighter and smiled, even though there were tears running down his cheeks.

The door to Jordan's room opened, and Bill and Alan Peters walked in followed by Mr. Timson, Mr. Campbell, and Mr. Allen. Jordan grinned with pleasure, quickly brushing the tears from his cheeks. Angelina slid her chair back out of the way to make room for the tall men to arrange themselves around Jordan's bed.

Everyone seemed to be talking at once, shaking hands, patting arms and generally rejoicing in the fact that Jordan was not hurt as badly as they had first feared. Angelina sat quietly, enjoying the back and forth banter between the men and Jordan and eating her sandwich. Suddenly she stopped to listen carefully.

Mr. Campbell cleared his throat. "So, Jordan, as of right now we're not pressing charges against Jason, unless you feel that it is really necessary." He glanced at Mr. Allen and Mr. Timson before continuing. "I realize that you and your mom may want to press charges, and if you do, we will certainly understand, but before you make a decision I would like you to listen to what Mr. Allen has proposed." Mr. Campbell looked at Mrs. Bradford for some sign to continue.

Jordan looked at his mother's stricken face, at the nervous twisting of the tissue in her hand and the quivering of her lip, and waited. Finally, she nodded her head in assent. Jordan turned to Mr. Allen, whom he trusted completely and said, "OK, Mr. Allen, what is it that you are proposing to do?"

Mr. Allen looked steadily into his eyes, and then said with a clear calm voice, "Jason, Travis, and Austin will be put on probation, and I will be in charge of their detention for the next four weeks. What I'm going to ask of you next may be hard to understand, but please hear me through before you respond. I want you to be in detention along with them."

Mr. Allen paused as Jordan laid quietly, a look of confusion and frustration on his face. The heavy silence in the room was almost like a loud roar in Jordan's head. Angelina slid her chair up close to the bed and placed her hand in Jordan's. He gripped it tightly, feeling strength flow from her hand into his.

"Hear him out, Jordan. I think I know what he is trying to do, and it just might work, but he's going to need your help."

Jordan turned to look at Angelina, and slowly a smile spread across his face. He glanced at his mother, who was staring with eyes wide with wonder as Sally Peters gently held her arm. Then he turned back to Mr. Allen. "All right Mr. Allen, I'll hear you out, and I'll do whatever you say. But just for the record, I trust you enough that even if you didn't explain why to me, I'd still do it."

Angelina wasn't the only one in the room with tears in her eyes.

After reassuring Jordan she would get all his homework and bring it over after school the next day, she hugged Mrs. Bradford, who held her very tight for a moment, and then, smiling through her tears, gently patted Angelina's cheek before turning to talk to Mr. Allen and Mr. Campbell.

Angelina walked between Sally and Bill to the car. Sally was holding her hand and Bill had his arm around her. Alan walked behind them.

Sally stopped by the passenger side door of the car and turned to Alan. "Want to come over for coffee and pie?"

"Thanks, but I think I'll head for home. I've got the dogs to feed and I'm opening up the shop tomorrow." Alan was two years older than Bill, but "Bill's Body Shop" was Bill's business. He was the "brains" of the operation, and Alan liked it that way. They did everything from oil changes and engine rebuilds, to bodywork and paint jobs. He liked the work and was happy to leave the headaches to his little bro.

"Don't worry Angelina, every thing is going to work out. OK? How about giving your old Uncle Alan a big hug?"

Angelina smiled up at him as his strong muscular arms embraced her. She slid her arms around him returning the hug. "Thanks for all your help, Uncle Alan."

Bill started the car as Angelina climbed in the back and shut the door. "See you in the morning, Alan. I should be in by 10:00."

CHAPTER EIGHT

SPECIAL NEWS

Angelina, Sally, and Bill were all deep in their own thoughts as Bill pulled away from the hospital for the five-minute drive home. The evening sky was clear and full of stars. The air was crisp with just the hint of frost. Most of the trees that canopied the street were still full of leaves in their rich autumn colors. As Bill turned the corner onto Center Street he glanced into the rearview mirror. "Well, young lady, you've had a rather exciting day today, haven't you?"

Angelina slumped farther down in the seat and closed her eyes, trying to hide from the day's troublesome memories. "More than I wanted. I really messed up today." Her voice broke under the stress she was feeling. A fresh wave of remorse and shame washed over her, and she covered her face with her hands and started to cry.

Sally turned her head to look back at Angelina. "Angelina, I told you that you didn't do anything wrong. We've all known this day was probably going to come sooner or later. We just need to figure out how we are going to handle it." She paused for a minute and looked at Bill. His smiling eyes that twinkled with excitement and the nod of his head gave her the encouragement she needed to continue. "Angelina, Bill and I have been talking, and we think it's time we told you something."

Angelina looked up at Sally, the panic she was feeling reflecting in the sudden brightness of her eyes. Bill and Sally rarely blocked their thoughts from her anymore, but she had been noticing for the last week there were times when she would come into the room and she knew they had suddenly blocked their thoughts from her. Sally had taught her how to block her own thoughts. She had somehow already known how to block other people's thoughts from her own mind. She did so most of the time out of courtesy to others. Blocking her own thoughts was not that hard or so different, once Sally had explained it. But now for some reason it seemed they were deliberately blocking her. Why? *They don't want me anymore! That must be it.*

Bill turned into the driveway, pushed the remote to open the garage door, and then pulled the car in. Turning off the motor he turned in his seat to look back at Angelina, his excitement of moments before masked by his concern for her thoughts. "Do you really think that we don't want you anymore?"

Angelina swallowed hard, her throat dry from the sudden onset of panic, and looked at Sally, who was looking at her the same way she had the first day she had met them. "I . . . don't know. You've started blocking your thoughts, and I thought maybe you were tired of me and didn't want to have to deal with me anymore." Tears were now streaming down her cheeks.

Bill and Sally both opened their doors and quickly got out of the car. Opening the back doors to the car, Bill squatted down to look at Angelina, and Sally climbed in and slid over in the seat to put her arms around her.

"Tired of you? Not want to deal with you anymore? Are you kidding? Angelina, we want to adopt you!"

Angelina stared first at one then the other. "Adopt me? Are you for real? You want to make me your daughter?"

Bill grinned. "Yeah, kiddo, we want to make it official, *if* that's OK with you."

"OK with me? Are you kidding? YES, YES, YES! Oh, it's very much OK with me," she said excitedly. Now she wasn't the only one crying. After a moment, Bill stood up and helped her out of the car. Sally climbed out the other side and shut the door.

Angelina paused for a minute and then said very hesitantly, "Would it be all right if I started calling you Mom and Dad?"

Bill looked at Sally who was now laughing and crying at the same time. "See, I told you she would want to call us Mom and Dad. Didn't I? Didn't I say she would? Huh? Huh?" Sally punched him in the arm and, putting her arm around Angelina, gave her a reassuring squeeze. "It is VERY much all right with us if you call us Mom and Dad."

Bill opened the back door to the house and held it open for Sally and Angelina, closing the garage door behind him. "We've already been talking to an attorney and have the paperwork almost done. We have a tentative court date, and if you're sure, we'll get it set firm so we can have this all done in about two weeks. How does that sound to you, Angelina?"

"Sounds too good to be true, *Dad*." She grinned at Sally, who was now laughing at Bill as he rolled his eyes at them both.

"So, who wants pie to celebrate?" Sally asked as she headed into the kitchen. Bill and Angelina followed her arm in arm.

Minutes later they were all sitting in the family room in front of a warm fire that Bill had started in the fireplace. Angelina swallowed a bite of pumpkin pie and looked up at Bill. "What do you think of Mr. Allen's idea?"

Bill looked at Sally for a moment before answering and then said, "I think it's going to be a little tough on Jordan, but if he puts his mind to it, well, it just might end up being the thing that will help Jason to make some changes in his behavior and possibly turn his whole life around."

Angelina sighed as she played nervously with her last bite of pie. "I know that Jason really respects Mr. Allen. If anyone can help him, I think it will be Mr. Allen. I really don't know what is bothering him. I've tried several times to read him, but I keep coming up against a wall of emotion: rage and hate. It really scares me sometimes. I was just thinking today that he was a ticking time bomb and that I didn't want to be around when it went off, and that's exactly what happened."

Sally set her plate on the coffee table. "I think I might know some of what it is bothering him. I ran into his mother, Ann. at the grocery store yesterday, and she was really struggling to get her shopping done. I could sense that she was in pain. She kept dropping things. When I followed her out to her car and offered to help put the bags in her car, she started crying. She found a lump in her right breast and is waiting to hear the results of the biopsy. They're afraid it's cancer."

"Jason's been mean for a long time. I don't think that's what's bothering him." Angelina took the last bite of her pie and set her plate down by Sally's.

"That's probably true, Angelina, but I'm sure this situation with his mother isn't helping." Sally stood up and reached for Bill's empty plate and the other plates to take to the kitchen.

Bill stood up and walked over to the fireplace. "George is a hard man, Angelina. He expects a lot of Jason, but he also puts him down a lot. No kid can take being put down all the time and not end up with some real issues." Bill poked the fire and little sparks flew up the chimney. "He needs a really good friend. Not a crony but someone who won't be intimidated by him; someone who will stand by him. I think Jordan could be that someone, given half a chance."

Angelina hugged her knees and stared into the fire. The red, yellow, and blue flames danced magically in and around the wood. She felt deliciously warm, happy, and content, yet she also felt apprehension for Jordan. It was going to be tough for him to go to detention with Jason, Austin, and Travis. He had not done anything wrong. They were the ones who beat up on him. But she knew what Mr. Allen was trying to do. She just hoped Jordan would be strong enough. "I'll help him as much as I can, but I know he's going to have to do most of it on his own."

"Just try to be a good friend to him, Angelina. That will be the best thing you could possibly do for him." She looked up at Bill, silently reflecting on what he had said, and then said thoughtfully, "Jordan has some issues of his own about his dad. I just don't want more put on him right now than he can handle."

Bill made sure the grate was secure in front of the fireplace. He was silent, as if deep in thought, then he said softly, "Ya know, Angelina, everybody has a hurt in them somewhere, and we each have a choice to let that hurt destroy us or to use the hurt to help us grow. I'm hoping Jordan will choose to let his hurt make him into a better man than his dad was. If he lets it consume him, it will end up destroying him, and he will discover that when he looks in the mirror, all he will see is his dad."

He stroked Angelina's head, and then continued, "You had a

pretty big hurt yourself, kiddo. Just think about all you've been through and still have to deal with on a daily basis. You're an amazing young girl, Angelina, and *your mom and I* are very proud of you!" He ruffled her hair as she sniffed and dried her eyes on her napkin. "Are you coming up to bed soon?"

"I will in a few minutes. I just want to sit here for a little longer." Alex came around the corner of the living room and, spying her, bounded over to rub against her, purring loudly. She pulled him into her lap and sat staring into the fire, listening to the soft murmur of Bill and Sally's voices as they headed upstairs to bed.

Remembering Bills words . . ."*Your mom and I are very proud of you.*" lifted her spirits. *Wow! Wait till I tell Jordan.*

Thinking of Jordan again, she shuddered anew, remembering how she had felt when she first realized he was hurt. She hadn't been that scared since the summer they were twelve years old and were spending their second summer up at the cabin at High Ridge with Papaw Jake and Mamaw Emma, Bill's parents.

High Ridge was the name of the valley up in the mountains where Jake and Emma Peters had a huge log home and barn on a lake. They owned the thirty-six acres surrounding the lake and had kept it wild and untamed. Angelina and Jordan had been going there every summer since they were eleven.

That second summer was the summer they seemed to continually get into trouble. She smiled, remembering how Jordan would come up with such crazy ideas that somehow always ended up earning them very special "jobs," from restacking the firewood pile, painting the rowboat, to picking up rocks out of the garden plot, and always, weeding and watering the garden. Their normal chores included cleaning out the stalls in the barn and caring for the horses and chickens. Angelina loved collecting the eggs, except when the hens were broody. She'd been pecked many times. She laughed, remembering the day Jordan had run screaming for the house when one of the roosters attacked him. Papaw Jake had come out with Jordan later; they cornered the rooster and in no time relieved him of his head. Mamaw Emma had shown Angelina how to pluck, gut, clean, and fry a chicken that afternoon, and they ate the bad-tempered rooster that night for supper.

She remembered well the afternoon that Jordan got hurt. The two of them had finished their chores early and were itching for something to do. Papaw Jake had promised to take them fishing but then had run to town on an errand, saying he'd be back before they were done with their chores. He hadn't gotten back before they were done, and they ended up climbing up into the loft to play in the hay. Papaw had told them not to go up in the loft, but Jordan talked Angelina into going up anyway, saying he was sure Miss Puss had some kittens hidden up there. Angelina knew the kittens were under the back porch but willingly followed Jordan up the ladder. They climbed the bales of hay for a while, but when a bat swooped down at them, Jordan's foot slipped on the ladder as he was trying to get down, and he fell to the barn floor.

It happened so fast that Angelina barely had time to try to stop his fall. Because she had never "lifted" anything as heavy as Jordan was, she couldn't hold him, and he fell hard the last three feet.

She would never forget his scream of fear and pain and then the silence that had followed. Mamaw was at the barn door almost before Angelina reached the bottom of the ladder. She'd cried as Mamaw checked Jordan out and then carefully "floated" him to the house. Mamaw put his leg in a splint and had him resting on the downstairs guest bed before he woke up. He never did ask how they had gotten him to the house.

Papaw Jake came home only to have to turn around and take Jordan back to town to get his leg set at the hospital. He was in a cast through the first week of school.

She'd been so scared. She had sat by the side of the bed that time too, holding his hand and crying. Just as he woke she let go of his hand, rubbing the tears from her cheeks. He had been in pain but had still been more concerned for her and apologized for the trouble he had caused. It was lonely the last two weeks up at the lake without him, but when Angelina had finally returned home three weeks before school started, she was over at his house most of the time.

Angelina slowly stood up, Alex meowing reproachfully at her as he stretched and jumped on the couch to curl up on a pillow. She scratched behind his ears and bent down to blow softly on his fur. His paw reached up and patted her chin. She laughed softly and then headed up the stairs to her room. Once in her room she walked over to the window to look out at Jordan's bedroom window across the driveway. It was dark. Almost always there was a light on or at least the glow of the computer screen could be seen as he played video games before going to bed.

A lump formed in her throat. She was going to have to give some serious thought to these feeling's she was having. Seeing him on the ground, unconscious, had really shaken her. What was it again that she had thought? *NO! NO! JORDAN!! OH, GOD, NO! Jordan! Oh, Jordan! Can you hear me? Jordan, please, you have to be all right. Please! I can't lose you!*

"I can't lose you?" It didn't take a genius to tell her that Jordan meant more to her than she realized. *I wonder how he really feels about me. What was it that he said to me at the hospital when I started crying?*

~ SPECIAL NEWS ~

"Don't cry, Angelina, I'm OK. It's gonna be all right! I'm NEVER going to leave you or do anything to put you in harm's way! Do you trust me?"

Angelina smiled, blushing in the darkness of her room, as she began to dress for bed. *I wonder what he meant when he said that.* She climbed into bed and pulled the covers up under her chin, their cool freshness pleasing to her hot face. She lay staring at the ceiling, listening to the different night sounds the house made.

The minutes passed slowly as she tossed and turned on her bed trying to get comfortable. Her mind could not settle down for going over the events of the day; first and foremost, Jordan being able to hear her talk to him in his head. Then there was the confrontation between Jordan and Jason in Creative Writing, followed by Jason being a jerk in the cafeteria. Then, of course, there was the whole fiasco in the pool and the argument that followed with Jordan in study hall. The horror on the football field still brought a cold chill to her heart. Jordan finally finding out he could hear her in his head was actually a relief. But best of all was Bill and Sally wanting to adopt her.

"Angelina, it's 2:00 in the morning. Honey, can't you go to sleep?" Sally's caring, gentle words stirred up Angelina's emotions anew.

Angelina turned over on her side and looked at the window. She sighed. *"I'm sorry, Sally, I'm trying to go to sleep. I just can't stop thinking. So much happened today, and, well, I'm feeling things that I guess I'm not sure I want to admit to feeling."*

Angelina felt a pressure on the bed, and turning over onto her back, looked up into Sally's loving eyes.

Sally reached over and stroked Angelina's hair.

"Honey, you're becoming a young woman. You've known

Jordan for a long time. You two are like two peas in a pod. You've been best friends for a long time; you've been through a lot, and well, your relationship might be changing." Angelina blushed, trying to keep her mind blank. "Honey, it's OK. It's all a part of growing up. Just take it slow, OK?"

Angelina sat up and threw her arms around Sally, giving her a hug. Sally hugged her back. Angelina started crying and clung to Sally. Sally held her, stroking her hair, silently reassuring her that everything was going to be all right. Angelina finally stopped crying. As she lay back she looked at Sally. *"I'm so glad you and Bill want to adopt me. I really love you guys."*

Sally bent over and kissed Angelina on the forehead. Suddenly she was not there.

"We love you too, Angelina. Try to go to sleep now. You have a big day ahead of you tomorrow."

As Angelina drifted off to sleep, her last coherent thought was: *I'm gonna have to get Jordan's study notes from his locker, and I was going to get his history notes after football practice!*

CHAPTER NINE

ANGELINA SHARES HER GOOD NEWS

Jordan was out of school the rest of the week. Jason, Austin, and Travis all walked around with long faces, and Jason sat on the bench for the whole game against the Hamilton Bullets Friday night. Mr. Timson did not change his mind and said Jason would have to sit out the next game too; however, he could play the last two games, but only if there was no more trouble. Their first detention was for Saturday morning at 7:30 in Mr. Allen's classroom. Jason was really mad about that.

Angelina had taken diligent notes in all their classes on Wednesday and dropped them off that night after school so Jordan could study. He would be making up his midterms starting on Monday when he officially came back to school. He was planning on showing up for the Saturday detention.

Angelina worried all day Wednesday about seeing Jordan for the first time since the night before at the hospital. Would he immediately start asking questions? She was not sure just how much she wanted to tell him, but she knew she could not lie to him anymore. That was one less thing she had to worry about. What could she say to encourage him about going to detention? He knew as well as she did what Mr. Allen was trying to do, but was he really up to it? *"Be a good friend,"* Bill had said last night. Well, she could do that, no problem.

Mrs. Bradford was all smiles when she opened the door to Angelina Wednesday after school. "Oh, Angelina, I'm so glad you're here. Jordan's been so restless this afternoon. I just told him he could get up for a while. I'll let him know you're here. I'm sure you can go right up."

She hurried up the stairs calling out to Jordan that he had a visitor. Angelina slowly followed.

"Who is it?" His voice sounded muffled, so Angelina figured he was pulling on a sweatshirt. His door burst open just as Evelyn and Angelina reached it. Jordan grinned happily at her as his mom fussed over his mussed hair and rumpled sweatshirt. She smiled back, feeling suddenly shy.

After several minutes of questioning, Evelyn left for the kitchen to prepare a snack for them, and they settled down on the daybed couch to look over all the notes and homework she had brought.

Jordan watched as she pulled out a set of notes she had made for each of their classes. She tried to stay focused on what she was doing, trying not to act nervous or self- conscious. Jordan finally reached over and caught her hand in his.

"Look, I don't want you to be nervous or worried about anything. I'm not going to ask you a whole bunch of questions. When you're ready, I know you'll tell me what you think I should know. But I think it's real neat what you can do."

Angelina looked up at him, relief showing on her face. "Thanks, Jordan. I have been a little anxious about all of this. I really do want to try to explain it all to you, but I just need a little time. What's more important to me right now is how you feel about going to detention. Are you really OK with this? I know you understand what Mr. Allen is hoping to accomplish, but are you really OK with it? Can you do it?"

"Yeah, I think it will be OK. I'm sure Jason is going to make a big deal about the fact that I'm in detention also, but I've made up my mind I'm not going to let it get to me." He picked up Angelina's notes for Mr. Allen's class. "Ya know, when we're in Mr. Allen's class, Jason is different. I almost like him. Maybe, if I start treating him as if he is different, he will be." He reached for his history notebook and opened it, glancing at what Angelina had written down and comparing it to some of his older notes. She smiled. Jordan really loved history.

Evelyn tapped on the open door and came in with a tray of tuna sandwiches, chips and a couple of Cokes. "Wow, Mom, that looks great!" Jordan stood up, taking the tray and set it down on the table in front of the couch. "Thank you, Mrs. Bradford, this really does look good." Angelina reached for a sandwich and Coke.

"You two eat up and I'll check in on you later. If you want more, just give a yell." Evelyn turned and walked toward the door. She stopped at the door and looked back, smiling. "Feels almost like old times," she said, then turned quickly to hide her tears and left the room.

"You've got a really great mom, Jordan. Don't ever do anything that will cause her any pain, OK? Please promise me, OK?" Jordan blushed knowing that Angelina was remembering Algebra class and his thoughts about shoplifting the Flight Masters video game. He opened his mouth to apologize when suddenly Angelina's face showed excited shock. "Oh my gosh! I almost forgot. How could I? You're never going to guess. Oh, I'm so excited to tell you I can't believe I haven't told you yet." Angelina was shaking with excitement.

"Well, are you going to tell me, or just sit there and vibrate?" Jordan laughed, his eyes smiling at her.

Angelina nearly exploded with her announcement: "Bill and Sally want to adopt me!"

Jordan stared at her, eyes large with amazement. Then he was hugging her and laughing all at the same time. Next he was holding her at arm's length and asking question after question without letting her answer. Laughing and brushing the tears from her eyes, she managed to say, "Slow down, Jordan. I can't answer all your questions at once."

He let go and leaned back on the couch in exhaustion. "Wow! This is way cool! I'm so happy for you, Angelina. When did they tell you they wanted to adopt you?"

"Last night, after we got home from the hospital; they knew I had had a really rough day, and I guess they thought that it would be a good time to tell me." Angelina took a drink of her Coke. "I have to admit, it sure helped make a bad day turn around into a perfect ending. I still can't believe it. They really want to adopt me!"

"Why wouldn't they? You're wonderful!" Jordan exclaimed, laughing as he reached for another sandwich.

"So what time did you get released from the hospital today?" She asked, reaching for some chips.

"Dr. Johnson came in to check me this morning at 9:00 and ordered one more x-ray, so I was ready when Mom got there at 11:30. They made me eat first, and we came around 1:00. I've been going nuts lying here in bed, so just before you got here Mom came up and said I could get up and get dressed." He stuffed the rest of the sandwich in his mouth and reached for his Coke. "I'm really glad you came over. Thanks, too, for taking such good notes in all the classes. I don't know why I can't go back to class tomorrow. I'm really going to be crazy by tomorrow night. You are coming over again, aren't you, and Friday too? Oh, wait, are you going to the game Friday night?"

"Well, that depends. I'll probably go to the game --" Angelina turned to look at Evelyn as she walked into the room with an armload of folded laundry -- "that is, if your mom will let you go too."

Evelyn turned to look at them. She frowned slightly and then looked first from one to the other. "OK, you can go . . .but, you have to dress appropriately and you have to promise to be careful and come straight home after the game; or, if you go somewhere with Angelina, Bill, and Sally, you have to call and let me know." She stood there with hands on her hips.

Jordan reached for Angelina's hand. *"She looks like a ferocious animal protecting her young, doesn't she?"* Angelina could feel the laughter in his thoughts. *"She loves you, Jordan. Promise her!"*

Jordan stood up, let go of Angelina's hand, and walked over to his mother. Giving her a big hug and lifting her off her feet, much to her protesting, he then set her back down and kissed her gently on each cheek. "You are the best little mother in the whole world. I love you, Mom, and of course I will do whatever you want. So relax, let me see that cute little smile. Come on, do I have to tickle you?"

Angelina watched the two of them, a smile of contentment on her face. Uncle Alan had been right; everything was going to be OK.

Thursday was a short day, with midterm exams in Physical

Science, MS Word/Business, and Algebra. Each class was an hour and ten minutes long for testing, with a ten-minute break between. Angelina was home by 12:15, and after eating lunch with Sally, went over to Jordan's to help him study. They actually got a fair amount done between talking about how grumpy Jason and his buddies were and Jordan's teasing for hints on the exams Angelina had already taken. Of course, they had to play video games on his computer too.

At 5:15 Angelina called Sally to ask permission to eat supper with Jordan. They worked on their Creative Writing essays till 8:00 when Mrs. Bradford poked her head in to say she was going to take a shower and go to bed. Angelina thanked her for supper and gathered up her papers to go home. Jordan walked her to the door.

"Thanks again, Angelina, for all your help with our studies. I'd be in hot water without you. You take pretty good notes in History when you have to!" He laughed as she tried to punch him in the arm. In the scuffle she dropped her Creative Writing papers. As they both stooped to pick them up their hands touched. Angelina felt her face flush hot with emotion. She stood up quickly waiting, as Jordan gathered up the scattered papers. Her own thoughts and feelings were so strong she totally missed Jordan's thoughts.

As he stood up and held out the papers to her, he thought; *I wonder what she would do if I kissed her?* He stood there silently watching her as he held out the papers. Finally he waved his free hand in front of her blank face and she jerked back to the moment. He grinned as she took the papers from him; thanking him for picking them up, she shuffled them around and put them back in order.

"No problem," he said softly, opening the door for her. "See ya tomorrow?"

Angelina waved back at him without turning around and ran

toward the house. *He must think I'm crazy! What is wrong with me?*

"There ain't nuttin wrong with you, Angelina. You are completely, one hundred percent, normal!"

Angelina could hear Bill laughing and Sally scolding him. *"Oh, Dad!"*

Friday was an even shorter day. She finished her Creative Writing term paper essay and then flew through her European History exam. She felt she had done well on both. PE was easy, with only five girls to be tested, including herself, and then she headed home.

Angelina changed into blue jeans, a sweatshirt, and cowboy boots and hurried over to Jordan's house. She sat in the kitchen with Evelyn while Jordan changed his clothes too. Then he grabbed his jacket so his mother wouldn't fuss at him, and they went back to Angelina's house to wait for Bill to come home and take them to the game.

Later that evening as they rode home from the game, they talked about how well Greg Burns had tried to hold the lead at the end of the second quarter. Unfortunately, the Hamilton Bullets had intercepted a pass, and their running back had run 42 yards to make a touchdown right at the end of the fourth quarter. The Indians had lost 8 to 12. Jordan was frustrated. They could not afford to lose too many games if they wanted to keep their lead and be able to go to the state playoffs.

Angelina watched as Jordan climbed the steps to his back door. Just before going in he turned and waved, grinning. Angelina sighed with relief.

CHAPTER TEN

FIRST DETENTION

Jordan walked down the deserted hall to Mr. Allen's classroom Saturday morning. The echo of his footsteps preceded his arrival. How quiet it was with no one else around. It was only 7:15. If at all possible he wanted to be in the classroom before Jason. Mr. Allen was sitting at his desk when Jordan opened the door and came in. The room was empty. Mr. Allen looked up and smiled, nodding to the four desks with maps on them. Jordan went over and sat at the desk farthest away from the door.

"Jordan, I just want to thank you for coming today. I really appreciate your willingness to go along with this." Mr. Allen stood up and began putting a small booklet on each desk. As he set the booklet down on Jordan's desk, Jordan scanned the title with piqued interest.

"SURVIVAL: Some Useful Relationship Values for Improving Victory at Living!" "Wow. This should be fun." Jordan looked up at Mr. Allen and grinned.

~FIRST DETENTION~

"I'm hoping everyone will take this seriously, Jordan. There's too much uncontrolled anger around here. We all need to work on relationship skills to try to get a handle on this." Mr. Allen glanced at the clock on the wall and walked over to the door to look down the hall. He stood there for a moment, then turned and walked back to his desk; sitting down, he reached for his notes and began reading them over.

The sudden banging of the outside door, loud laughter, and periodic banging on a locker door heralded the arrival of Jason, Austin, and Travis. The noise stopped abruptly as Jason entered the room and spotted Jordan sitting at his desk. With a snicker he asked, "What's *he* doin here?"

Mr. Allen stood up, walked over to the door, and closed it behind the boys. "Please take your seats. Jordan was in the altercation that took place on Tuesday, so naturally he would be here also. Please sit down; no, not in the back, Travis, take one of the three remaining seats up front here. Any seat with the map and booklet on it will do."

Mr. Allen stood by the side of his desk, arms folded, and waited for the boys to settle down. Once it was quiet,

Mr. Allen cleared his throat. "Before we get started, I want to set a few ground rules. For every fifteen minutes you are late, one Saturday will be added to the end of your detention time. Each Saturday we will be spending one hour here in school and then out to my place to spend another hour. The last detention will be on Friday night, after the game, instead of Saturday morning, and it will be an overnight hike and camp out. The hour that we are here in school we will be going through the small booklet on your desk and also learning how to read a map and some other physical survival techniques, besides the survival techniques for relationships. Any questions?" All four boys sat with open-mouthed, deer-in-the-headlight expressions on their faces.

Austin was the first to recover from Mr. Allen's amazing announcement. "Ya mean we're gonna learn about survival and then actually go camping?"

"What's '*survival techniques for relationships*' have to do with camping?" Travis was flipping aimlessly through the booklet.

Jason's eyes narrowed as he looked Mr. Allen in the eye. *What's his game? All this sissy stuff about re-lay-tion-ships! They should have to deal with my old man, then they'd see just how awful relationships can be.* Jason absently rubbed his face where his dad had struck him that morning when he didn't get out of bed fast enough to please him.

His dad, George Morton, owned and operated the only gas station in town. Jason resented this because it meant he spent most of his Saturday's and three to four nights a week helping out at the station. Yeah, his old man paid him, but it was an "under the table" payment at a measly $55 bucks a week and he still made him pay for his own gas.

He was forever on his case about school, football practice, and working at the station. It seemed like nothing he did was ever good enough. He shifted uncomfortably in his chair; still hurting in other areas of his body from the beating he got Tuesday night. The old man had gone ballistic that night over his being pulled from Friday's game and possibly from the last three games. He had ragged on and on how scouts were out looking over the schools for possible players, and if he wasn't careful he was going to miss his chance to really make something of his life. Jason shook his head in frustration. If it weren't for his mom, Ann, he'd have cut out a long time ago.

Jordan glanced at Jason, then looked at Mr. Allen and asked,

"What will we be doing for the hour we are at your place each Saturday?"

Mr. Allen did not take his eyes from Jason as he answered Jordan's question. "Well, I have a lot of yard work to get done before the snow flies, and you'll be learning how to start a campfire and put one out, put up and take down a tent, use an ax, find drinkable water, tie knots, and climb; just to name a few." Jordan grinned with pleasure.

Jason sat very still, eyes locked with Mr. Allen. *OK, maybe it isn't a game. Maybe this won't be too bad.* He glanced at Jordan, who was now studying the map on his desk. *I wonder why he's really here.* Looking back at Mr. Allen, Jason thought for a moment he saw a look of sorrow in his eyes and then it was gone. He cringed involuntarily remembering the look in his older sister's eyes Tuesday night and again this morning when she'd brought him a bag of ice for his face.

He really did respect Mr. Allen and hated being in the mess he was in. Sighing, he looked back up at Mr. Allen and said, "OK, Mr. Allen, I guess I'm up for being your cheap labor for a few weeks. Don't know for sure what this '*relationship*' stuff is going to do, but hey, maybe you-all will realize what a really great guy I am and cut me some slack." Austin and Travis joined Jason laughing.

"Maybe," Jordan paused for a second, still looking at the map, "maybe when this is all said and done, we'll all understand the uniqueness of each one in the group and the value each brings to the whole and find some common ground on which to build some lasting, substantial relationships without feeling our own person and space is being mocked or threatened."

Everyone was quiet for a moment, as if soaking up what Jordan had just said. Suddenly Travis laughed nervously. "Wow,

Jordan that was some sermon!"

"Shut up, Travis!" Jason barked harshly. He turned to look at Jordan, who was now looking at him with a look of sad, resigned pain in his eyes. Jason had the feeling Jordan was not trying to be smart. *We're each unique and we each have value, and we have some common grounds? I'm gonna have to think about this.* Jason turned back to Mr. Allen. "OK, Mr. Allen, I'll do more than just put in my time. I'll give this a shot."

Mr. Allen sighed with relief, and picking up the booklet, opened it to the first page. "OK, let's get started. Take about ten minutes and read the first four pages in the book. Then we will talk about what the word 'relationship' means to each of us."

Seeing each boy pick up his book and start reading was rewarding to Mr. Allen and raised his hopes. *Yes, yes, yes! This just might work.*

Less than an hour later, as they all piled into Mr. Allen's Land Rover, they were still debating the different meanings of 'relationship' and had more questions about the final detention hike/campout. Mr. Allen was content to see a slight, subtle change in the three boys' attitude towards Jordan. It wasn't that they were being condescending, or even accepting of him. It was more like they were seeing him in a different light. They all knew that Jordan's dad had just taken off one day and had not been heard from until two weeks ago, when his mom had been served with divorce papers. They each knew the hard times he and his mom had been through, and yet here he was, going through this just the same as they were. He had thoughts and ideas and feelings too, and he did not seem to walk around with a chip on his shoulder or think the world owed him something.

Mr. Allen was not expecting a complete, unconditional

bonding after the first day, but he felt the first hour had gone very well. He could sense the beginnings of an attitude of respect for Jordan from the other boys. Plus, everyone seemed to be trying real hard not to mock anyone's ideas or feelings or cut anyone down.

On the drive from Baker's Bluff to the farm Mr. Allen pointed out the different farms and sights. He told the boys how he had inherited his farm from his father, who had inherited it from his father. Mr. Allen's grandfather had come from another country to settle the mountainous acres around the small settlement of Baker's Bluff, before it was even a town. History buff that he was, he talked about how Baker's Bluff had gotten its name from the man who had seen the meteor fall back in 1882, Mr. Jonathan Baker, and how the settlement had popped up overnight due to the mining of the metal found in the meteor site.

As they passed Old Mine Road that led to the mine, he commented on how there wasn't much mining going on at Henderson Mine Works anymore, which was probably why Baker's Bluff had never really grown. There were only a handful of families now in Baker's Bluff who had lived there for several generations. It was, for the most part, a quiet, friendly town.

Jordan looked at the sign they passed-"Baker's Bluffs"-which was for the fairly large ski resort two miles down the road. He smiled remembering the many wintry Saturdays he'd spent up on the slopes with Angelina, Bill, and Sally. He'd never been to any of the several hunting lodges in the area since he always went hunting with Bill and Alan up at High Ridge.

He'd been thinking a lot lately about the different enterprises the town offered, as he wanted to get a job so he could save up for a car by next fall. He knew he did not want to work at any of the restaurants or either of the motels in town. He knew that kind of work would have him climbing the walls in no time.

Baker's Bluff Lake was great for swimming, boating, and fishing, which contributed to the continuous flow of tourist traffic year around. Baker's Bluff Campgrounds was on the lake too, so he'd gotten certified in first aid and lifeguard safety and rescue over the summer in hopes of landing a job with them for next summer.

Jordan stared out the side window, thinking about their small town of 1200 residents. His mom worked for Richard Briggs, who owned and operated the *Baker's Bluff Daily Times*. It was a small paper, but Mr. Briggs did a pretty good job keeping everyone up to date on all of the local news and most of the state and national stuff. He'd thought about going over to Baker's Bluff Public Library and talking to Marney's mom, Heather Burns, and asking her if he could work some evenings at the library. He knew it was open most evenings till 8:00, but he also knew Mrs. Burns had some local seniors who worked part-time for her too, so he wasn't sure if she would really have a need for him.

Suddenly Travis's laughter caught his attention. He was teasing Austin about his questioning why they could not just ride in Mr. Allen's Land Rover to a campsite instead of hiking, and what kind of wild animals were there where they were going to be hiking? Jason was patting Austin on the head, saying in a soothing voice, "There, there, Austin, it'll be all right. We'll protect ya. We won't let any 'Big Foots' get ya!" Travis was holding his sides, snorting with laughter.

Jordan grinned for a moment as Jason and Travis mercilessly teased Austin. They seemed to be such good friends. He looked at Travis, who was a good five feet nine inches tall, built just like his dad, William Andrews. His twin sister, Katie, looked a lot like their mother, Elizabeth. Jordan shuddered involuntarily, thinking how weird it would be to have parents who ran a mortuary business. He did not like thinking about death or dying.

Jordan laughed as Austin took off his hat and threw it at Travis. Austin had copper-red hair, just like his mother used to have. He swallowed hard, remembering when the news had reached the school halls the previous year that she had passed away after a long battle with lung cancer.

Austin's dad, Jonathan Thomas, owned and operated Thomas's Hardware, and had smoked like a chimneystack for years. He'd quit smoking, cold turkey, the day his wife, Mary, had been diagnosed with lung cancer. Jordan knew Mr. Thomas was still struggling over the loss of his wife. Austin was too. He helped his dad most afternoons after school and Saturdays at the store. Jordan had gone into the store on several occasions to get things he needed to make different repairs at the house, and had seen how the two of them just seemed to be lost. It was good to see Austin laughing and having fun, even if it was in detention.

Jordan glanced at Jason and shifted uncomfortably, remembering his original plans for Tuesday night. From what Mr. Allen said, Charles Baker, who owned Baker's Books and Stuff was actually the Great-great-great-grandson of Jonathan Baker. Baker's Books and Stuff was a combination bookstore, music store, video games, and video movie rental all in one. He blushed slightly as he suddenly realized that if it hadn't been for Jason, Travis, and Austin ganging up on him at practice that day, well things could really have been a lot worse than they were.

He turned to look back out the side window. The need to find a job consumed his thoughts again. About the only other businesses in town were the Baker's Bluff House and Home, which sold everything from toasters and bed sheets to beds, dressers, TV's and freezers, and Belinda's Clothing Shop. Belinda's Clothing Shop and the Second Time Around shop, run by Jennifer Hill, Abby's mom, were the only places in town to get clothes and shoes. Actually the Baker's Bluff Bible Church ran the Second Time Around shop. Rev. Duane Hill was the pastor, but his wife, Jennifer, had the shop open two afternoons a week. The other three afternoons she gave piano lessons. There was literally no chance of getting jobs with any of those places and besides; it wasn't really what he wanted to do anyway.

There was also Baker's Bluff Cannery, which employed a fair amount of the local residents, and was owned and run by Robert Henderson, whose great-great-great-grandfather was a brother to Mr. Alexander Henderson, who started Henderson Mine Works. He could possibly get a job there this coming summer if the campgrounds job fell through. Henderson Mine Works was still operational and was currently being run by Daniel and Joseph Alexander, both, great-great-grandsons of Alexander Henderson, although they weren't getting nearly as much out anymore, but he could try there too.

He was pretty sure that Angelina was going to try to get a part-time job with Albert Jenks, the town vet. He was also in charge of the animal shelter, so he was sure to need some help.

Jordan glanced over at Jason, who was laughing at Travis, who was now insisting that relationships had to do with things being the same, like fruits and vegetables, and beef and chicken. They were basically the same, in relationship to each other. Jordan grinned as Jason grabbed his side, laughing. Suddenly their eyes met. Jordan nodded, continuing to grin. Jason grinned back, then turned to look outside as the Land Rover turned into a long, tree-lined drive.

At the end of the drive stood a huge farmhouse with a porch that wrapped around the side of the house. There was a new three-stall garage, and farther back there were outbuildings and a very large barn. Chickens were wandering around, and out in the pasture he could see cows calmly grazing. The door off the side porch opened, and a large Border collie came bounding out to greet them. Mrs. Allen came out to stand on the porch and watched as they all climbed out of the car.

While Travis and Austin were petting the dog, both Jordan and Jason looked at Mr. and Mrs. Allen with a sense of hopeful longing. Mr. Allen had closed the door of the Land Rover and turned to look up at his wife, a content happy smile on his face. He waved and then turned to the boys, laughing: "OK, guys, now the real fun begins!"

As the five of them headed toward the barn, Jordan and Jason both paused to look at each other. Almost, as if in silent agreement, they each held out a hand to the other. Grinning at each other, they clasped hands, then, letting go, walked side by side toward the barn, trying to anticipate what the next four weeks held for them.

~

Angelina glanced at the clock on her nightstand. One o'clock. Where could he be? They should have been back at least two hours ago. Jordan did not know how to block, so she was not sure why she was having difficulty at least hearing his thoughts. Or Jason's, or Austin's, or Travis's for that matter, and she could almost never catch Mr. Allen's. Why was that? Walking over to the window, she looked out at Jordan's house and sighed. Scratching her head, she returned to her desk. *I wonder why it is that I can hardly ever hear Mr. Allen's thoughts.* Suddenly she heard a car pull into Jordan's drive.

"Angelina! I'm back!"

Angelina was out of her room and pelting down the stairs

almost before Jordan had finished his thought. Bill, standing at the bottom of the stairs, caught Angelina as she tripped down the last few steps. "Careful, little girl, you don't want to break that pretty neck!" Bill grinned at the back of her head as she bolted out the front door. Sally poked her head into the hall from the kitchen. "Did she almost fall again?"

"Yeah." Bill walked into the kitchen and slipped an arm around Sally's waist, giving her an affectionate squeeze. "Do you think we're headed for trouble with Jordan knowing Angelina can read minds?" Bill snaked a finger full of chocolate chip cookie dough from the bowl Sally was mixing up. She playfully swatted his hand, and then turned to look at him. "I don't know. I hope not. What do you think?"

Bill stood silently, listening to Angelina and Jordan's excited voices, and then looked at Sally. "I think I need to have a talk with Jordan. Maybe try to explain a few things to him. How much I tell him is really the issue. My gut says I can trust him with our lives, which is what I will be doing if I tell him, but I still feel hesitant. What if, in a rash moment, he lets something slip? I just don't know, Sally. I just don't know."

After Sally finished dropping the cookie dough by rounded teaspoonfuls onto the baking sheet, she put it in the oven and set the timer. She turned to look at Bill. "You know what happened in the hospital with Evelyn when Jordan agreed to do what Mr. Allen asked him to do, don't you?" Bill looked at her and sighed. "Yeah, have you talked to her since? How is she taking it?"

Sally reached for both their coffee cups and went to the coffeepot to refill them. "I actually talked with her this morning after Jordan left for detention. She's obviously curious as to why we can do the things we do." She paused to cup her hands around the now chilled coffee and heated it up till it was steaming. "But she actually seemed relieved to know we're not witches or demons. Just normal human beings who happen to be able to do extraordinary things that she could probably do too, if she had as high a level of ATP in her cells and as active a brain as we do." She turned to hand Bill his cup and then proceeded to heat hers.

Bill grinned as he took the cup. "And she bought that?"

"We don't know that's not the reason. Our ATP levels are off the chart, Bill." Bill leaned over and kissed her on the cheek. *"We don't know it IS the reason, either!"*

The front door burst open, "MOM! DAD! Jordan's back; wait till you hear what happened. It's soooooo cool." The excitement in her voice made them laugh, but that wasn't what brought tears to Sally's eyes. Bill put an arm around her as she hurriedly brushed the tears away. Bill felt the lump in his own throat. Angelina had slipped so easily into calling them Mom and Dad that they were actually feeling guilty they hadn't made the decision to adopt her sooner. She certainly left no doubt how she felt about the whole thing.

The timer went off on the oven. "Come in the kitchen for hot cookies and milk and you can tell us all about it," Bill called out as he went to the cupboard for glasses for the milk while Sally went to get the cookies out of the oven.

Angelina and Jordan came walking into the kitchen, grinning from ear to ear. "Wow, Mrs. Peters, those smell really great! I shouldn't be hungry; Mrs. Allen fed us all before she would let Mr. Allen bring us back to town. She had fried chicken, mashed potatoes and gravy, corn on the cob, and fresh cherry pie. It was awesome." As he reached for some cookies he grinned at Sally's raised eyebrows. "Well, I've ALWAYS got room for YOUR cookies!"

Bill laughed as he took the plate of cookies from Sally and

set it on the table and then poured both Angelina and Jordan some milk.

"So, tell us all about it, Jordan. How'd it go?" Sally started spooning her next batch of cookie dough onto the baking sheet.

Jordan told them how Jason, Austin, and Travis had arrived at class and how they had all agreed to be respectful to each other; about the discussion on what "relationship" meant to each of them; and how it seemed everybody was trying really hard to get along and not to pick on each other. He told about the ride out to Mr. Allen's farm and how he and Jason seemed to come to a silent agreement to give each other a chance. He talked about how neat the farm was, the animals, the barn with a rope in the loft, and how they had ended up climbing the rope and swinging and dropping into the hay. How they had all worked hard together to clean out the stalls for the cows and then practiced making knots. Mrs. Allen had fixed them a great lunch and made them feel like family, hollering at all of them, including Mr. Allen, to wash up for lunch, and to leave their "dirty shoes" out on the back porch. "We don't live in the barn, ya know!" Jordan smiled thoughtfully, shaking his head. "It sure wasn't like any detention I've ever gone to before. I don't think Jason and I are going to be immediate best friends, but I do feel a little more hopeful about what we are trying to accomplish."

"It sounds like you had a good beginning, Jordan. I'm really proud of you. It couldn't have been easy this morning, not knowing how it was going to turn out." Bill paused for a second and then continued. "I just don't want you to get your hopes too high too soon. Jason acting one way, with just his two buddies watching is one thing: acting that way with the rest of the school watching may be another whole ball game. Just be careful. Give him time to see just who you really are. Give him a chance to take the bait. I have to agree with Mr. Allen that I think there is hope for Jason, but I think a lot will depend on you." Bill looked at Jordan, holding his gaze with a compassionate smile. *"I think you're up for this, Jordan, but just remember, if you ever need anything, all you have to do is call out to me. I'll hear you. I'll be here for you. OK?"* Jordan looked at Bill, eyes wide with wonder, and nodded his head.

"So," Bill said, punching Jordan playfully in the arm, "you gonna let your mom know you're alive and well, or are you going to keep her fretting for another hour?" Jordan jumped to his feet, alarm showing on his face. "Oh, I almost forgot. She's probably worried sick! Thanks for the cookies, Mrs. Peters. I better run." As Jordan reached the kitchen door, he stopped. Slowly he turned and looked back at three of the most important people in the world to him. *"You all mean the world to me. Thanks for believing in me. I hope I don't ever let you down."*

Sally walked over to Jordan and took him in her arms, hugging him; then she held him at arm's length. *"You are very precious to us, Jordan. Don't you worry; we won't let you let us down. We will always be here for you and your mom."* "Now, go on home and let her know you're OK. We want both of you to come over for supper later, say around 5:00." Kissing him on the cheek, she turned him around and gently pushed him out the kitchen door. She stood watching him as he let himself out the front door and sprinted across the lawn to his house.

Sally turned back to the kitchen to see two grinning faces looking at her. "What? Hey, can I help it if I really dig this mothering thing?" There was much laughter and happiness as the three of them worked together to fix a feast fit for a celebration.

CHAPTER ELEVEN

MEMORIES AND CONCERNS

Jordan sat impatiently drumming his pencil on the desk. He had arrived at school early and had gone straight to Mr. Walters' Physical Science class. He had not been able to get Mr. Peters' words out of his head. *"I just don't want you to get your hopes too high too soon!"*

Jordan had struggled going to sleep Sunday night, trying to figure out all the implications of Bill's statement. He had only fallen into a restless sleep after coming to the decision that he wanted his first encounter with Jason to be in a classroom full of kids and a teacher, and not in the hall at his locker or on the way to school. He actually had not waited to walk to school with Angelina; that in itself was almost unheard of, but he had let her know he was leaving early and why.

The fact she could know what he was thinking was very amazing to him. They still had not talked about it very much, and he was anxious to know how she did it. Knowing that Sally and Bill could also read his thoughts blew his mind.

Jordan's shoulders visibly tensed as he sat on the stool at his science station, staring out the classroom window, thinking back to the first time he met Bill and Sally Peters. He had just turned ten. He and his folks, Norm and Evelyn, had moved to Baker's Bluff that summer. His dad owned a small airplane and did local crop dusting and short distance charter flights. His dad had taken him for an airplane ride for his birthday. Jordan had been so proud of his dad. He wanted to be a pilot, just like him. *Just like his dad.* Jordan clenched his fists and shook his head in angry frustration.

He remembered the day like it was yesterday. He'd been so excited to be going flying with his dad. They had spent almost an hour up in the plane. They had flown over the town and the mine and even the canning factory. His dad had told him how he would be flying more as he would be doing more charter flights for the owners of the factory and the mine. He'd just sealed the deal that morning. That was why he had been late picking up Jordan to take him to the airport. They flew over the mountains and had come back a little later than they had planned, but it had been so much fun. Jordan knew what he wanted to be when he grew up: a pilot, just like Dad.

He could not wait to get home and tell his mom all about it. How his Dad had let him hold onto the copilot control stick. How he could already explain about the horizon on the control panel and all about air speed.

When they had turned onto their street, the ambulance in the driveway surprised both him and his dad. His dad had parked in the street out front and was out of the car almost before it stopped moving. Jordan knew something bad must have happened. Paramedics were bringing his mom out of the house on a stretcher when his dad reached the door. He kept saying her name, over and over. Sally and Bill were following the paramedics as they came out of the house, and Bill started explaining to his dad that his mom had called them just minutes after they had gotten home to say she had fallen. They had come right over; they knew at once the fall was causing her to lose "the baby," and they had called the ambulance that was now taking her to the hospital. *The baby?* Jordan had not even known that he was going to have a baby brother or sister.

Bill had taken Jordan's dad, Norm, to the hospital, while Jordan stayed with Sally. He remembered her being kind and not asking him a lot of questions or even trying to tell him everything was going to be OK. She had just made cookies and asked him to help her.

Bill brought Norm home several hours later. His mom was going to be OK, but Jordan was not going to have a brother or sister, ever.

His dad went straight into the house. Bill came in and told him what had happened. His mother had apparently lain unconscious for over an hour before she came to and called Bill and Sally. Something happened inside her that could not be fixed and now she would not be able to ever have another baby. Jordan had tried not to cry. He remembered how Sally held him in her arms, trying to comfort him without saying anything. After a while Bill walked him across the lawn, trying to explain that his dad was not mad at him, just mad at what had happened. But nothing was ever the same after that day.

Two weeks later Angelina had come to live with Bill and Sally. They became friends almost immediately. Their bedroom windows faced each other across the driveway. There was a huge tree in the back yard that was right on the fence line. Bill and Jordan had been talking for a few weeks about building a tree house in it and they started it the first week Angelina was with them. It was awesome. It took them almost two months to completely build it, but when it was done you could get to it from either yard. Building the tree house and spending almost all his free time with Angelina, Bill, and Sally, Jordan had been able to pretend that everything was OK at home. He was able to not see the sadness in his mother's eyes, or notice his dad was always gone, flying more and more charter flights.

Then his dad left.

One morning he got up, drank the coffee Mom always had ready for him, took the lunch she always had packed, and walked out the door. Nothing had really seemed any different that morning from all the other mornings since Mom had come home from the hospital. No, nothing was different except he never came home.

At first they feared maybe his plane had crashed. They waited for news. But there wasn't any. No call, nothing. He was just gone. Chief Waits had checked with the airport and with the people who chartered the flight the day he left. There was no crash. Then, their bank account was emptied. They finally had to accept the fact he had left them and was not coming back.

For a long time Jordan blamed himself for his mother losing the baby and for his dad leaving. If his dad had not taken him flying on his birthday, maybe Mom would not have fallen and then he would have a little sister or brother, and Dad would still be here with them and they would be a happy little family. He remembered how two years ago he finally broke down on his birthday and told his mother how he felt. He would never forget the pain and sadness in her eyes.

He remembered how she grabbed his arms and shook him and then held him tight, sobbing. They sat up late that night talking it out. She told him it was not his fault she lost the baby. She already had been having some problems. What had happened between her and his dad, well that was not his fault either, and he'd just have to trust her on that matter.

Thinking back, Jordan knew the last five years had not been easy. Mom had finally gotten a job at *Baker's Bluff Daily Times.* She did not make a lot, but Jordan helped by mowing lawns, shoveling snow, and painting houses and garages. Things were tight, but they were OK. Mom was almost finished with her first novel and would be sending it off soon to a publisher who had liked her story line and was working with her through the writing process. Once it was published, and if people liked it and bought it, well, maybe things would be a little easier. Even though they were doing OK, Jordan still resented his dad leaving and destroying their "home."

Now Mom had received papers from an attorney in another state, papers saying his dad had filed for a quick divorce, and it would be final once she signed and returned the papers.

Jordan didn't realize his hands were clenched into tight fists until he felt soft, gentle fingers on his own. He felt Angelina's caring thoughts before he turned to look into her compassionate eyes. *"Your mom really is handling this whole thing a lot better than you know, Jordan. She's starting to get her 'happy' back!"* Angelina smiled at Jordan's grin. Getting your 'happy' back had been his mom's way of keeping him from pouting too long when he could not do something he wanted to do.

"How long have you been here?" he asked, relaxing his hands and reaching to pick up the broken pencil he had unknowingly snapped in two.

"Not long *here,* but I've been *with* you ever since you started reminiscing." She searched his face for some sign of acceptance and then, shrugging, slipped onto the stool next to his. "Sorry."

Jordan glanced around the room; Jason hadn't come in yet. "It's OK," he whispered. "I'm kind of glad you can be *with* me. I wish I could get past all of this. I mean, it's been five years; you'd think I could let it go and get on with my life. I guess it's just I hate what he's done to Mom, to us. I hope I don't ever have to see him again. I'm not sure what I would do if I did." Jordan glanced at Angelina to see her reaction to what he had just said.

She was silent for a moment and then turned to look into his troubled brown eyes. "I do know how you feel, Jordan; I really do understand. This hasn't been easy for either you or your mom. But I believe all of this has made you both stronger. Holding onto bitterness over what your dad did to you and your mom will not change the past, but it will affect your future, and you have to know that it would not be for the good." She stopped for a moment to let what she said sink in. Then reaching for his hand she continued. *"The effect it will have on your future will be to turn you into a bitter angry man, just like your dad. It will only hurt you, your mom, and those you are closest to."*

Jordan sighed and shook his head. "I'm sorry, Angelina. I am trying."

"I know you are, and I know how hard this has been on you. I'm proud of you, Jordan."

Just then the door burst open, and Jason, Austin, and Travis came sauntering into the room. The bell was ringing, and Mr. Walters was already handing out an outline with the week's lesson plan. Jordan and Jason's eyes met and held for a moment. Jordan nodded slightly. Jason gave a short bark of a laugh and headed for the stool next to Amy. Travis and Austin took the ones in front of them. Jordan turned to face the front. Well, at least Jason had not yelled some smart remark at him. Maybe it was going to be OK. Jordan opened his book and tried to concentrate on what Mr. Walters was saying about the periodic table.

As Jordan dressed for the game Friday he was thankful for a fairly uneventful week. He knew he was going to sit on the bench the whole game, but he hoped his being there would give the team some moral support. Dr. Johnson told him Thursday at his checkup he wanted him to wait one more week before getting back into the game. Jordan was frustrated with not being allowed to play yet, but at least he would be able to play for Homecoming the following week.

It had not been an easy week even though it had been fairly uneventful. Jason was not out rightly being his usual smart aleck self, but every now and then something he would say or do gave the impression he was being stretched to the limit of his good behavior. Monday through Wednesday, Jordan spent his study hall and one hour after school making up the midterm exams he'd missed the week of his injury. After his checkup on Thursday with Dr. Johnson, he decided to dress for Friday's game, even though he would not be playing.

Jordan and Angelina had walked home after the game, choosing not to join the rest of their friends at the local pizza shop. They had lost by a field goal; Jordan was not in the mood for pizza, and he was dreading detention the next morning. He tried to explain to Angelina the frustration he was feeling, wondering if Jason was only acting like he was trying to change. If it was all an act, then the whole thing was a big waste of time.

Walking home from the game, Angelina tried to be encouraging to him, but he just was not in the mood to be encouraged. Suddenly Jordan became aware Angelina was no longer walking beside him. Stopping, he looked around. *Now where did she go?*

A small twig hit the top of his head. Looking up, he saw her sitting on a limb a good ten feet up in the tree. His mouth dropped open in surprise. "How'd you get up there?"

Glancing up and down the deserted street, Angelina carefully slipped off the edge of the limb and gently drifted back to the ground. Jordan's eyes were large and his face paled slightly. He swallowed hard and took a step backwards.

"You weren't listening to me, so I had to do something to get your attention." She watched him carefully for signs of panic.

"OK. OK. So, you've got my attention. You want to explain what just happened?" His voice shook even though he was trying desperately to sound calm.

Angelina sighed. "Let's go to the tree house." Jordan looked at her outstretched hand. Slowly he put his hand in hers. "OK." They walked the rest of the way home not talking out loud.

"I don't know or understand completely why we can do all the things we can do. Bill said it has something to do with the meteor that fell here back in 1882. Bill and Sally have been slowly teaching me how to use and control the abilities that I have. They can do a lot more things than I can, but I am learning more stuff all the time and will eventually be able to do all the things they can do. Bill said it wasn't important for me to know and understand everything right now. I will, as I get older. I really don't think about it that much. I guess I'm just glad to know I'm not some freak from outer space or something."

Angelina glanced at Jordan, who had been staring straight ahead as they walked along, his eyes large and round with wonder. He was still somewhat taken aback whenever she would talk to him in his head.

~ CHAPTER ELEVEN ~

They stopped walking at the driveway leading to Angelina's house. "You still want to go to the tree house?" She had let go of Jordan's hand. He stood there staring at the house and then looked at Angelina. "Yes I do, that is, if you still want to."

Angelina smiled and then took off running for the back yard, laughing. "Race ya!"

"Hey, that's cheating!" Jordan yelled, starting to run to overtake her. He stopped short, staring in disbelief as he watched her run. One minute she was running up the drive, the next she was standing on the platform of the tree house, waving down at him.

Oh my gosh! How did she do that? Movement at the kitchen window caught his attention. Sally and Bill were standing at the sink, looking out at him. *"Don't be scared, Jordan. It's OK."* He shook his head and shut his eyes. When he opened them he was shocked to find he was standing beside Angelina on the platform of the tree house. She grabbed his arm to keep him from stumbling backwards and falling out of the tree. Her eyes were dancing with excitement. *"So, how much more do you want to know?"*

Jordan sat down so he would not fall, trying to calm the mad thumping of his heart. Looking down at the house, he could see Bill and Sally standing in the doorway that opened onto the deck. Bill had an arm around Sally. He waved and then they turned and walked into the house out of sight.

Suddenly Jordan was laughing with excitement and let out a loud yell. "Wow! That was so cool. Did they do that or did you?" As he stood up, he turned and looked at Angelina, her smiling eyes twinkling with pleasure. They walked inside the tree house and sat down on the cushions on the floor. "They did. I can move myself and smaller items, but I'm not up to moving another person just yet." She reached over and tapped a small light bulb that she had just hung that day from the roof by a string of twine. It started to let off a pale glow. Jordan watched, his eyes round with wonder. A box slowly drifted down from a shelf, and Angelina opened it and took out an apple, handing it to him.

"You sure you're not from outer space?" he asked, laughing, and rolled off the cushion away from her as she tried to punch him in the arm. He stopped and looked at her. "Hey, remember last week, when you jumped in the pool and saved Amy? Everyone said it looked like you were in a bubble or something. What was that all about?" He crossed his legs and started eating the apple.

"I can create a kind of protective shield around me. I think it's a combination of energy, coming from me, and molecular matter that's already in the air. See?" Jordan could just make out a slight glow around her. Slowly he stretched out his hand. It came up hard against what felt like plastic. She grinned. Just as quickly, the glow faded and he fell forward from the absence of the shield. He caught himself and looked up at her.

"Wow. This is amazing stuff. The scientific world could sure have a field day with you!" The look on Angelina's face made Jordan wish he could take back the words and thoughts he had just had. He choked on a bite of apple, struggling to apologize for his words and to relieve the anxiety that showed in Angelina's eyes. "Look. I didn't mean anything by that. You know your secret is safe with me. I don't want anyone taking you away and doing all kinds of weird tests on you." He paused, scratching his head and giving it a quick shake. "Hey, wait a minute. This feels kinda weird. It's like I'm speaking someone else's thoughts."

"You were. They were from Bill. That's what would happen, you know. They would take us away and study us; they'd try to figure out why and how we do what we do. It would be awful, Jordan.

People in general don't like it when other people can do things that are considered 'unnatural.' It scares them, and usually they react before thinking or asking questions. Situations can escalate out of control before you know it, and then somebody is almost always hurt." Angelina's voice held a note of sadness and acceptance. The look in her eyes was one of sad resignation. "We can help you forget all of this if you think it's too much for you to deal with."

Alarm exploded in Jordan's mind. *"NO! NO! I don't want to forget. I said your secret was safe with me and I meant it. Please, Angelina, please, Bill, please believe me. Sally? Sally, you believe me don't you?"*

Jordan rubbed his eyes hard with his hand. When he looked back at Angelina he was shocked to find himself sitting cross-legged on the back deck of his own house. He scrambled to his feet.

"Listen, Jordan. Things have been moving fast, maybe a little too fast for you. Please know and believe this: we do believe in you, and we do trust you. But, we need you to understand the seriousness of this. We're going to have a family conference tonight and we'll talk to you tomorrow, when you get back from detention. Don't worry. It's all going to work out."

Jordan knew it was Bill talking to him. He stood there looking up at the tree house, a lump in his throat. *"Don't worry, Jordan, Angelina wants you to know that she believes you, and she's not upset with you. OK?"*

Jordan sighed, and turning, went into the house. She believed him. That was all that mattered.

CHAPTER TWELVE

SECOND DETENTION AND A MISUNDERSTANDING

Jordan arrived early again the next morning for detention. Mr. Allen was writing on the blackboard and did not stop writing or look at him as he entered the room.

"Good morning, Jordan. Please take the same seat you had last week."

Jordan sat down and looked at what Mr. Allen had written on the board.

```
     values
     n: beliefs of a person or social group in which
they have an emotional investment (either for or against
something); "he has very conservatives values"
     1) Please make a list of what you consider your
        five most important personal values.
     2) Read pages five to eight in the "SURVIVAL"
        booklet.
```

Jordan opened to page five and started reading. He was almost done when Jason, Austin, and Travis came walking in. Jordan glanced up and was disheartened to see Jason looking as if he was ready for a fight. Jason did not smile or nod at Jordan, which was even more discouraging. He sighed and looked back at his book, trying to refocus on what he had been reading.

Mr. Allen waited for the boys to be seated and then directed their attention to what he had written on the board, saying he would allow them twenty minutes to do the assignment and then they would discuss their lists.

Jordan sat with his pencil in hand, staring at the blank piece of paper in front of him. What were his personal values? What were his beliefs? What did he have an emotional investment in? When he closed his eyes, he could still see the sad look of resignation in Angelina's eyes. Jordan swallowed hard and started writing.

Values

1. Honesty
2. Trust
3. Following through - sticking to your word
4. Giving someone second, third, fourth chances
5. Never giving up

Jordan laid his pencil down and picked up the booklet to finish reading page eight of the assignment. When the twenty minutes were up, Mr. Allen stood up and asked for a volunteer to read his five values.

No one raised a hand. Travis snickered in his hand, but did not volunteer. Mr. Allen calmly waited, looking at each boy. Finally, Jason pushed his chair back roughly and stood to his feet. "OK, you want to know what my values are; fine. One: don't ever turn your back on anyone. Two: don't believe what anyone tells you because most likely they're lying to you. Three: take care of numero uno because no one else will. Four: do whatever it takes to get ahead. And last but not least, number five: don't be a fool by letting your emotions show."

"Amen!" Austin snorted. "Ditto," Travis echoed.

~SECOND DETENTION AND A MISUNDERSTANDING~

Mr. Allen was silent as he calmly eyed the boys. Then his gaze moved to Jordan. Jordan shifted uncomfortable as he saw Mr. Allen's right eyebrow rise as if questioning him if he had a comment.

Jordan glanced at Jason and was surprised to see him calmly eyeing him with what looked like expectation.

Jordan cleared his throat. "Well, I guess I could tell you my five values." Glancing down at his paper, he cleared his throat again with a slight cough. "I guess I would have to say that honesty, being truthful, in what I say and do is probably my first and most important value. Then I would say trust, in myself, in my friends and family, and people that I look up to. Umm, then I guess, following through with what I have made a commitment to do, sticking with something or someone, ya know, seeing it through to the end, sticking to my word. Then, I guess, giving people second, third, fourth chances, however many it takes. Lastly I'd have to say never giving up, not on my dreams, not on my goals, not on my plans, and not on my friends."

"Ooooh, now that statement should get you a gold star, Jordan-boy." Travis laughed, rocking back on his chair. Jason kicked at the leg of the chair and Travis went sprawling on the floor.

"Shut up, Travis. I didn't hear *you* opening up and sharing your values with the group." Jason turned to look at Jordan. "That took guts, Jordan. I have to say, I'm impressed." He sat nodding his head, speculation in his eye. Jordan watched Jason, trying to decide if he was being serious or getting ready to say something smart, when Jason suddenly continued. "Listen, when you say you'll give people second, third, and fourth chances, does that go for your old man too?"

Jordan felt the color drain from his face. His hands clenched the sides of his desk. *"Jordan, take a slow deep breath! Try to relax. Don't let him push you into reacting."*

"Bill? Jordan felt a tingling sensation all over his head.

"Just relax and take a minute to really think about what he just asked you in relation to what you said were important values to you. Be honest with yourself, Jordan."

Jordan looked up at Mr. Allen, trying to get his eyes to focus. Mr. Allen was watching him, calmly, waiting for his response. Jordan turned to look at Jason.

"I don't know, Jason," he finally said in a hushed, halting voice. "That's a good question. I guess I haven't really thought about the whole 'second chances' thing in relation to my dad. I don't know what I would do if he came back." Jordan felt his body beginning to relax, and feelings he had been ignoring now came to the surface. "Sometimes I think I hate him and would like to beat the crap out of him. Other times I think that maybe if I had been different, you know, smarter, or better behaved, maybe he wouldn't have left us. Sometimes, I just feel sick. Why did he leave? Why?" Jordan now looked directly at Jason. "And sometimes, I think if I saw him again, I'd be afraid. Afraid I'd cry. Afraid I'd beg him to stay, to not leave us again. I think I'd promise him anything, if he'd just love me again and if things could be like they used to be."

Silence settled heavily over the room as the full impact of Jordan's words reached each of the boys. Travis had gotten up off the floor and was now staring at Jordan, just as Austin was. Neither said a word. Jordan finally sighed, and shaking his head, he looked at each of the boys, ending up with Jason. "Well, now would be a good time to laugh and make fun of me if you're going to. A chance like this probably won't come around again, at least not for another half hour or so."

~SECOND DETENTION AND A MISUNDERSTANDING~

Jason continued to stare at Jordan, his face pale. He swallowed hard and finally said, "I'm not going to make fun of you." Jason glanced over at Mr. Allen who had not moved and seemed to be waiting for him to finish. "So, ya gonna give me another chance?"

Jordan gave a short, soft laugh, shaking his head. "Sure, Jason. Second, third, fourth, whatever it takes."

Mr. Allen, who had been sitting on the edge of his desk, stood up, and clearing his throat, he looked at each of the boys. "I think we'll cut this short and head out to my place. Any of you ride horses? I have a section of fence that needs to be fixed, and I thought we'd ride horses out to the spot. Then we're going to set up and take down a tent and start a fire--no matches." He grinned as the boys exchanged excited nods and grins.

Five minutes later they were all in the Land Rover heading out of town. Travis and Austin kept peppering Mr. Allen with questions about his horses, while Jason and Jordan sat in the back. Jason was silent, shifting uncomfortably in his seat. He finally turned to Jordan. "Look, I'm sorry about what I said back at school. I was way out of line. We all know how hard it's been on you and your mom. My sister's always saying my mouth is as big as it is because I keep sticking my foot in it. I guess I was just in a rotten mood 'cause of my own old man. He's really riding me hard about screwing up and not being allowed in the game last night or last week. We lost last night and last week, all because of me. I'm such a jerk. You get to play next week, don't you? Mr. Timson said last night after the game I could play for sure next week."

Jordan grinned. "Yeah, I get to play next week. I felt sorry for Greg last night. The Jackson Rockets defense guys were on him all night long." Jason nodded in agreement. "Listen, about back there in school, it's OK. I should be thanking you. Your question made me stop and think and finally face up to some feelings I've been trying to ignore for a long time. Not that I think my dad's coming back, but I really need this to be a closed issue."

Jason was silent for a moment, staring at his tightly clasped hands. "I hate my dad sometimes too," he said in a hushed voice. "And other times, I guess I'm afraid too, and I think I hate that even more." Jason looked up at Jordan. "Do you think it's a no-win situation?"

Jordan thought hard and fast and then said very softly, "Look, Jason, no matter what your dad says or does, he's still your dad. He may not know how to show you, but I think he does care, you know, love you. But he's only human; he's gonna make mistakes. I don't think kids are born with a book for the parents to read telling them how to raise the kid or how to be good parents. It's kind of a hit and miss sort of thing, ya know?" Jordan paused for a moment. Jason waited silently for him to continue. "Just be open to talk to your dad. When you approach him, remember he's not perfect and accept him for who he is. Always tell him the truth, even if you know he's gonna want to beat the crap out of you. And let him know you respect him. You might be surprised; things just might turn around."

Jason continued to sit with his hands clenched in tight fists. "Nothing I do is ever going to be good enough for him!" Resentment filled his voice.

"Just do your best, Jason. Most important, be honest first with yourself and do your best, for your own sake. Then show him respect, and I think you'll see a change. Trust me." Jordan felt the little tickle in the back of his mind like he had felt the night before up in the tree house with Angelina and wondered if he was getting some help with what he was saying.

~SECOND DETENTION AND A MISUNDERSTANDING~

What was really strange was he was actually surprised to find that he believed what he was saying.

Jason looked up at him and grinned. "OK, Jordan. I'll give it a try."

Jordan smiled. Hope. It was an awesome thing.

When Mr. Allen dropped Jordan off at his house he discovered that no one was home at the Peters. As he walked back over to his house kicking a stone, he suddenly "knew" they were out grocery shopping. He scratched his head, grinning, and after giving his mom a quick hug and kiss, hurried upstairs to play a video game. It was a good two hours later that Jordan was still sitting at his desk playing video games when the phone rang.

"Jordan! It's for you; it's Angelina!" Evelyn yelled from downstairs in the kitchen. Jordan reached over his stack of books and picked up the phone, not taking his eyes off the computer screen, and still working the control with his right hand.

"Hi, Jordan, what are you doing?" Evelyn hung up the kitchen extension.

"Don't you already know?" he teased and then sighed as the "game over" screen flashed up on his computer. He leaned back in his chair to look out the bedroom window.

Angelina waved, smiling. "I think you're playing a video game. I get really strange thoughts from you when you are doing that."

He laughed. "So, what are you doing?"

"I'm talking on the phone to you, silly!" Jordan loved to hear her laugh. "So, do you want to come over? Bill just went to pick up a movie. Sally and I are making pizza and popcorn."

Jordan jumped up and turned the game off. "I'll be right

over!" He hurried down the stairs and went into the kitchen where his mom was folding towels on the table. "Mom, is it OK if I go next door? Bill's getting a movie and Sally's making pizza and popcorn." Jordan stood there watching his mother carefully fold a bath towel.

"I can't believe you're hungry already, after that big lunch Mrs. Allen fixed for you boys again." She set the towel aside and picked up another one to fold. She turned to look at him. "Everything OK between you and Angelina?"

Where did that come from? "Sure, why do you ask?" Jordan walked toward the back door and reached for his jacket hanging on a hook.

Evelyn stopped folding the towel. "Well, you were kind of quiet when you came in after the game. You came in so early I knew you hadn't gone to get pizza with your friends like you usually do; and you went straight to your room."

Jordan put his jacket on and stood with his hand on the doorknob. He turned and smiled at his mother. "I guess I was a little bummed by our losing to the Jackson Rockets last night. Plus, I knew I had to be up early for detention." He waited, looking at his mother's furrowed brows. Finally he let go of the door and walked over to her. Picking her up, much to her protesting, he twirled her around. "Everything's OK, Mom, so don't worry!"

As he set her down, she slapped playfully at his hand, then held onto his arm, her eyes searching his face. "Honest, mom, everything's OK." He bent and kissed her on the cheek.

"OK, go eat pizza. I'm going to finish up this laundry and then go work on my book. It should be ready to send to the publisher by the end of next week. Have fun. Don't forget your key, and don't be too late." She picked up the folded towels and headed for the bathroom.

~ SECOND DETENTION AND A MISUNDERSTANDING ~

Jordan grabbed his keys off the hook by the door and slipped out, locking the door behind him. He ran across the drive and around to the back door of the Peters' house. Angelina opened the door just as he stepped up to the porch. Jordan jumped back, startled, and then stood shaking his head at her as she laughed.

"Come on in, Jordan," Sally called from the kitchen. "Angelina, you're going to scare the life out of him if you aren't careful." Sally bent to put the pizza into the oven.

Angelina smiled. "Come on, Jordan. I'm making popcorn; you can help me."

"Help you make popcorn? How hard is it to make popcorn? Don't you just put a bag in the microwave and push a button?" Jordan hung his jacket up on the hook by the back door.

"No, we have this old-fashioned popper that we use in the fireplace. It makes really good popcorn." Angelina picked up the tin of popcorn, the peanut oil, and the big wooden popcorn bowl and headed for the family room where there was a nice fire burning in the fireplace. She set everything down on the stone hearth next to the popper and then tossed a couple of pillows on the floor and sat down on one. Jordan dropped down beside her, watching her with interest.

Angelina picked up the popper and handed it to Jordan. "Here, you hold this and I'll put in the oil and popcorn."

He held the popper while she flipped open the top and poured in a small amount of peanut oil and then two handfuls of corn. She then snapped the lid shut and opened the grate in front of the fireplace. "OK, now hold it in the flame, but be sure to keep it moving. We'll soon have really delicious popcorn!" Jordan grinned at her pleasure over something as simple as popping corn. He quickly turned his attention to the popper when he heard the first kernel pop. In no time it was popping like firecrackers going off on the Fourth of July. When the popping stopped, Angelina opened the popper with some hot pads, and Jordan dumped the white fluffy corn into the big wooden bowl. The smell of the freshly popped corn along with the smell of the pizza drifting in from the kitchen made Jordan's stomach growl and his mouth water with anticipation. Mrs. Allen had made them another great lunch, but that was hours ago.

Jordan watched as Angelina again poured in peanut oil and corn. Again he held it in the flame, keeping the kernels moving, listening for the first pop of the corn. He tried to keep his mind focused on what he was doing and not think about the direction the conversation during the evening was most likely to go. He glanced sideways at Angelina. She sat hugging her knees and staring into the fire, seemingly preoccupied with her own thoughts. *It's unfair that she can hear my thoughts anytime, but I can only hear hers if I am touching her.* He had to hold the popper with both hands, so he could not reach out to touch her. As the popping became more furious, Jordan again focused his attention on the popper. As it stopped, he pulled it from the flame and turned to Angelina. She was still staring into the fire. Resting the popper on the stone hearth, he was able to reach out one hand and very gently touch her arm.

"Jordan's friendship and trust is so important to me. I want so much to be able to help him with Jason and with his own feelings of insecurity and the anger he feels toward his dad. I think Bill is right. What Jordan said about our abilities was purely innocent and didn't mean anything. I know we can trust him. I feel it!"

"Angelina, do you really trust me?"

Angelina suddenly jerked and turned to look into Jordan's questioning eyes.

~ SECOND DETENTION AND A MISUNDERSTANDING ~

"How . . . ?" Her eyes fixed on the popper being held by Jordan's one hand, his other hand still on her arm. She raised her eyes to his. *"How could you listen in when you knew I was so deep in thought?"* She pulled her arm away.

Amazement showed on his face. "How could *I* listen in? What do you call what you've been doing? And if my friendship and trust is so important to you, and you want to help me with all these things I *need* so much help with, why are you getting bent out of shape over me listening to you? Are you for real or is this just some big game you're playing?"

Jordan had now let go of the popper and was standing up, staring down at her, hurt and frustration showing on his face.

Angelina jumped to her feet, her eyes flashing with anger. "I didn't *sneak* listen. I . . .I just couldn't help hearing. I was trying to help you! You were just trying to find out what I was thinking about."

Jordan slapped himself in the forehead. "Oh, stupid me, what was I thinking of? Trying to understand the *great* Angelina and hoping I hadn't messed things up. Well, maybe there isn't anything *to* mess up!"

"I'm *NOT* bent out of shape! You just startled me. And I am *NOT* playing some game! How could you even think that? And who says there *is anything* for you to mess up anyway?" Angelina was now shouting in anger.

Jordan's face registered shock and sadness. "Well, if there's nothing for me to mess up, then why is my friendship and trust so important to you?"

Angelina opened her mouth, but nothing came out. Tears suddenly filled her eyes. Jordan's anger and frustration instantly broke. He had not made her cry since he had snapped the head off her Barbie doll the day after her tenth birthday. He took a step toward her. She was crying hard now, her body shaking with her sobs. He took her gently in his arms, as she buried her face in the front of his shirt. *"I'm so sorry, Angelina."*

"No, I'm sorry."

"You're right. I shouldn't have sneaked to listen in. It's just I've been feeling so anxious about what I said Friday night."

"No, I had no right to snap at you. You're right. I have no room to talk. I can listen in to you anytime, and it's not fair for you."

"You didn't mean it, did you? What you said, that there isn't anything for me to mess up?"

"No, of course I didn't mean it. You know I'm not just playing games, don't you?"

"Yea, I trust you, Angelina. I trust you with my life!"

As they stood there staring at each other, they became aware of Bill and Sally standing in the doorway of the kitchen. "So . . " Sally asked, a funny little smile twinkling in her eyes, "is the first big fight over with? Can we eat this pizza before it gets cold and watch the movie, or do Bill and I need to go back in the kitchen for a while?"

Bill slipped around Sally and walked over to the T.V. tray and set the cans of pop down. "Sally, quit teasing them and bring the pizza. I'm going to get the movie set up." *"You two OK now?"*

Jordan and Angelina both nodded and then turned back to the fireplace to empty the popcorn into the bowl. "So, what movie did you get, Bill?" Jordan asked as Angelina carried the bowl of popcorn into the kitchen to pour the butter over the top. Jordan carefully closed the grate in front of the fireplace.

"Stephen King's <u>The Shining</u>!" Jordan grabbed his sides, collapsing on the couch, laughing as Angelina yelled from the kitchen, "Oh, come on, Dad, you didn't really get that one, did you?"

"No. I got the Disney movie you wanted. Now, come on, you two, I'm ready to start this thing."

Sally and Angelina came in carrying plates, napkins, glasses, the popcorn, and the pizza. Minutes later they were all comfortably munching pizza as they watched the previews before the movie.

Jordan looked at Angelina, sitting next to him cross-legged on the floor, their knees touching, and smiled. *"I really do trust you, Angelina. Do you trust me?"*

Angelina smiled and glanced at Bill and Sally, who were both looking at her. *"Trust you? Why, only with all of my heart, Jordan; only with all my heart."*

CHAPTER THIRTEEN

SECRETS, HURT FEELINGS, AND A MAKEUP

Jordan sat in study hall, across the table from Angelina. She was working on her Algebra assignment. He was supposed to be working on the Creative Writing essay assignment that Miss Fisher had given them that morning, but he couldn't seem to keep his mind on his writing. He kept thinking back to Saturday night at the Peters', after the movie.

They had talked till well after midnight. Bill explained how important it was not to draw attention to their abilities. It wasn't that they were trying to hide something or that they were "evil." They had just found from experience that most times when anyone discovered that someone could do something no one else could do, something "not natural", well, many times there were unpleasant ramifications. He did not explain in great detail why or how they could do the things they could do, just that it had something to do with the meteor that fell in 1882, just like Angelina had said. He had reassured Jordan they were not weird aliens, and when the time was right, he, Bill, would explain everything to both him and Angelina. She had seemed satisfied and content to wait, so he would too.

Jordan stared at Angelina's long, soft, curly hair. She kept pushing it back behind her ears as she bent over her math paper. She paused from working on a problem to look up at him. Jordan was looking at her but not really seeing her. She sighed. *Why is he thinking about my hair?*

"Pssst!" Jordan's head snapped, and his eyes suddenly focused on Angelina's face as she whispered, "What are you writing about for your essay?"

Jordan picked up his pencil and started drumming it on his book. "Something around the idea of 'what if' I saw my dad again. Why? What did you write about?"

Angelina leaned over her paper and whispered, "I wrote about being adopted. Did I tell you we have an appointment with the attorney next Tuesday afternoon? I'll be leaving school that day at lunch. I'm really nervous. We'll be setting a date for the adoption proceedings. I'm worried something will come up to keep it from happening."

"Don't borrow trouble, Angelina; nothing's going to go wrong. I don't think Bill and Sally would have set this in motion if there was even the remotest chance things would go wrong, or that you would be taken away from them. ***That's just not going to happen!*** OK?"

Angelina smiled, trying to feel reassured. "OK." Jordan chewed on his eraser as he continued to sit staring at his paper. He looked up at Angelina, who was almost finished with the Algebra assignment. He leaned forward and whispered, "So, are you going to the dance with me or not?"

She didn't look up and kept on working the math problem but whispered, "You still going as Peter Pan?"

"Yeah."

"Well, I guess I can be your Tinker Bell." She covered her mouth to keep from laughing out loud.

Jordan reached for her arm. *"Are you going to fly around my head?"*

Angelina laughed this time. *"I could. You know, if they were giving prizes for the best costume act, we'd win for sure!"*

Jordan jumped up as the bell rang and started stuffing papers into his backpack.

"Are you going to go and watch the practice again?" Angelina asked as she put her papers in her Algebra folder.

"Yeah, I still can't play till Dr. Johnson clears me after my appointment tomorrow after school. We have to win this Friday and next if we want to be in the state playoffs." Jordan swung his backpack over his shoulder. "See you after practice?"

"OK." Angelina sat and watched as he walked off toward the door.

"Hey, girl, you gonna go watch the guys practice again?" Abby hopped up on the table, swinging her legs as Angelina started to pack up her backpack.

"Hi, Abby; yeah, I guess so. Jordan can't play yet, not till after he sees Dr. Johnson tomorrow, but he'll still be there. So, I guess I'll go for moral support." She grinned as Abby put both of her hands, overlapped, over her heart, rolled her eyes, and swayed back and forth. Angelina shook her head, picked up her backpack, and started for the door. "You're a real comedian, Abby; come on, let's go."

Once out on the bleachers, Angelina and Abby didn't even pretend to be doing homework. They sat drinking Cokes, laughing, and talking; now and then they waved at the guys. The marching band was practicing in a small area off the west end of the field, the drums and cymbals challenging the trombones and trumpets. Abby saw Tony Reed and waved. Tony was fun and interesting; he was always telling wild stories about his dad, Michael, who was an EMT. His mother, Pamela, worked at the Baker's Bluff Library with Heather Burns. She always had information on the newest and hottest books that came into the library.

Abby turned to Angelina. "Tony asked me to go to the dance with him. We're going as an old man and woman. Did Jordan ask you yet?"

"Yeah, just a little while ago, in study hall. He's still going as Peter Pan, so I guess I'm going to go as Tinker Bell." She laughed. "I was going to go as Wendy, but I found out that's who Amy is going as. Jason's going as Captain Hook! That sounds appropriate, doesn't it?"

When Abby didn't answer, Angelina looked over at her. Abby was fidgeting with her backpack. "What's wrong?"

"I'm not sure, but I think something is wrong with Jason's mom. I overheard Mom and Dad talking about it last night. I think it might be serious." Abby paused, zipping and unzipping the front pocket on her backpack. "Do you think that could be part of the reason Jason's been so mean lately?"

Angelina was silent for a moment, thinking about what Sally had told her two weeks before about Jason's mom maybe having breast cancer.

"I guess so. It's just that Jason has been mean for so long. Maybe I'm being too hard on him. Jordan seems to think he's starting to change. I just don't know. Guess I'll have to see it for a while before I really believe it."

"So, I guess things are going pretty good between you and Jordan?" Abby asked, continuing to zip and unzip the pocket of her backpack.

Angelina blushed, pushing her hair back behind her ears. "Yeah, I guess so. It's strange; Jordan and I have been friends for over six years, ever since I came to live with Bill and Sally. Lately, it seems like he's more than just 'Jordan, who lives next door'." Angelina looked over at Abby, who was still looking intently at her. "I guess when he got hurt a couple weeks ago, I realized how important he is to me. Do you think I'm being goofy?"

Abby smiled. "You're going to be sixteen in four weeks, right? Is it going to be 'sweet sixteen'?"

Angelina sighed, blushing again. "Do you think I'm weird because I haven't been kissed yet?"

Abby's eyes became large with alarm. "Heck no, I think it's cool! I personally think that first kisses have been greatly underrated. I think a first kiss should be a momentous occasion, a landmark in the timeline of one's life. A first kiss should be so special that you never forget it; so wonderful that you just somehow know this is the only person you will ever kiss again. How cool is that? It kind of makes that first kiss really important, ya know what I mean? So, no, I don't think you're weird at all."

Angelina turned to look down where Jordan sat on the bench watching the practice. He sat straight on the bench, his broad shoulders tense with emotion, and his head turning from side to side, closely following the play. She turned back to Abby and squeezed her hand, and then released it. "Thanks, Abby. You're the best!"

Abby glanced down at Jordan. "So, Jordan thinks detention is going OK? I still can't believe they made him go to detention at all! He didn't do anything wrong. It was Jason, Austin, and Travis who were in the wrong."

Angelina was silent for a moment, trying to decide just how much to tell Abby. "Can you keep a secret?"

Abby's eyes glistened with mystery. "You know I can. What's up?"

"Well, Mr. Allen asked Jordan to come to detention. He didn't tell him he had to go. He ***asked*** him. I guess he thinks there's something in Jason worth saving. I think he's hoping Jordan will be a good influence on him or something. Well, I know that Jordan can be a good influence on anyone. I just don't know if Jason will be receptive or not. I think for Jason's sake he better be. We'll have to wait and see how it all turns out. I just don't want Jordan hurt."

Abby took a drink of her Coke and then looked off down the field at Tony. "So, I guess Jordan has decided you aren't keeping any secrets from him." She waited as Angelina choked on the sip of Coke she just taken and then continued. "How long are you going to keep me in the dark?" Abby turned and looked back at Angelina. "I thought we were best friends. I tell you everything, Angelina. Why won't you trust me?"

Angelina's mind raced as she cleared her throat. "Look, Abby, you know I trust you, and yes, we are best friends. You're my 'almost sister' for crying out loud!" She paused, trying to think how to reassure Abby without being insulting. "Abby, I just have a lot of stuff going on right now. I need to work a few things out. I promise

~ CHAPTER THIRTEEN ~

I'm really not keeping a deep dark secret from you. I just need a little time to figure something out and then I'll tell you everything. I promise."

Abby sat silently staring at Angelina, her hands clenched.

"Come on, Abby. Don't be mad. Let's talk about the dance. Did you know Greg Burns is coming as Indiana Jones? You know Jill Morton is going to the dance with him, don't you? I guess she's going to dress as a kind of female Indiana Jones. I really think that Greg and Jill will be voted in as the King and Queen, don't you?" Still Abby did not answer.

Angelina slumped forward, putting her head in her hands. "Come on, Abby. Please don't be mad." She looked up when she heard Abby get up, pick up her backpack, and start down the bleachers. She called out, "Aw, come on, Abby. Don't leave!"

Angelina watched as Abby slowly walked down the side of the field toward the band. "*Sally! This isn't fair! I HAVE to be able to tell Abby!*"

Jordan called Angelina Tuesday afternoon when he got home from his appointment with Dr. Johnson.

"I can play in Friday's game!" he roared with excitement. Angelina jerked the phone away from her ear. Sally, cutting up potatoes at the sink laughed, enjoying his excitement. "Congratulations, Jordan!" she yelled.

"Did you hear that? You were so loud I had to hold the phone away from my ear. Sally heard you clear over by the sink!" Angelina laughed.

"Sorry, Angelina, I'm just so excited. So, is Abby talking to you yet?" he asked, his voice suddenly gentle with concern.

"No. She avoided me all day, and it's really starting to bother me," she answered, trying to keep the emotion out of her voice.

~ SECRETS, HURT FEELINGS, AND A MAKEUP ~

"Mom's fixing fried chicken; do you want to come over for supper?" he asked enthusiastically, trying to cheer her up.

She looked over at Sally, who winked and nodded. "OK. See ya in a few."

Angelina walked over to Sally and slipped her arm around her waist. "Thanks, Mom!" Sally smiled then let out a yell as Angelina tickled her and took off running for the hall. *"Have fun, honey; don't be too late, you've got school tomorrow."*

Jordan was waiting on the front porch for her when Angelina came up the steps. "So why is Abby mad at you anyway?"

Angelina drew a deep breath. "Well, it's a long story. Remember the day you got hurt at practice? You were upset with me in study hall because you knew I was keeping a secret from you. Remember? Well, Abby came up to me after study hall that same day and wanted to know what we were fighting about." Jordan opened his mouth to interrupt, but Angelina rushed on. "So I told her you had some weird idea that I was keeping a secret from you. When we got out on the bleachers she started in on me too about keeping a secret. Then you got hurt and well, you know the rest of that. So, anyway, today she says, 'Guess Jordan doesn't feel you're keeping any secrets from him anymore. How long are you going to keep me in the dark?' I want to tell her, Jordan, really I do, but Sally and Bill think I should wait."

Angelina sat down on the porch step, kicking at the leaves that were swirling around on the ground. The cool autumn air made her pull her sweater tight about her shoulders.

Jordan sat down beside her, his muscular frame and soothing voice an inviting oasis of comfort she longed to turn to for rest and strength. "Listen, Angelina, don't worry, Abby isn't going to stay mad at you forever. I don't think she's really mad anyway. I think she's just disappointed. I know I was. I had always told you everything, and I could tell you were holding something back. It made me feel like you didn't trust me, and that hurt. But now that I know, well, I can understand why you didn't say anything. I probably would have done the same thing."

She did not look up but continued to kick at the leaves. Jordan reached over and took hold of her chin, turning her face so she had to look him in the eye. "Personally, I think you can't go wrong telling Abby anything. She's someone you can trust. Think about it. Talk it over with Sally, um, I mean your mom. It'll be OK."

He stood up quickly and pulled her to her feet. "Let's eat. I'm starved." As Jordan held the door for her, Angelina walked into the house feeling happier than she had all day.

~

Abby continued to avoid Angelina the rest of the week. Her happy feeling from Tuesday night was long gone by Friday afternoon, seventh period, when she and Jordan met up with the other students who were setting up the gym for the dance later that night.

By the end of the period, the gym had been transformed into a wonderland of delight. The gray metal bleachers had been folded shut into the wall so the entire gym floor was available for use. Small round wooden tables were arranged in double staggered rows around three sides of the gym. Artificial trees, five to six feet tall, were interspersed between the tables. Each tree was covered with white Christmas lights. On each table was a small carved pumpkin with a candle inside it; Indian corn and colored artificial leaves surrounded the pumpkin. The tablecloths were alternately orange and black.

Hanging from the ceiling at the center of the gym was a

round motorized crystal ball. With all the lights out except for the four spotlights on the ball, the room was sure to become a magical wonderland of delight. Orange, black, and white streamers hung from the ceiling, giving the illusion of constant movement. It was truly an awesome sight.

At the north end of the gym was the stage that held a DJ booth; which was connected to the large speakers in the four corners of the gym. The east end of the stage was set up for pictures to be taken. Center stage was the band. They were going to have a mixture of music played by the DJ, and live music played by the pop band made up of a group of kids in school.

Jordan walked Angelina to her locker after the bell rang. "I think the gym looks really great. It wouldn't if your mom hadn't helped. I'm glad Mr. Campbell was willing to let her go around and get donations. I hope we win the game tonight. It'll kinda put a damper on things if we don't." Jordan looked at Angelina to see if she was listening. "Abby still hasn't come around?"

Angelina stopped at her locker and started working the combination on her lock. "No. Jordan, what am I going to do? I can't stand this!" She spun the lock again in frustration when it wouldn't open. Jordan reached over and quickly dialed her combination, opening the lock. "It's gonna work out, Angelina. Don't worry."

She opened the locker door and turned to look up at Jordan, tears in her eyes. He caught hold of her hand, his questioning thought filled with concern, *"Are you going to be OK?"*

She smiled, brushing the tears from her cheeks with her free hand, *"Yeah, thanks. I'll see you at the game. Sally and Bill are going to bring us home after the game to change and then Bill will take us back to the dance. Is that OK with you?"*

~ CHAPTER THIRTEEN ~

Jordan tenderly brushed a stray tear off her cheek. "Yeah, it's fine with me. I really need to run now though; last practice before the game. You sure you're OK?"

"I'm fine. Go on." She watched him run down the hall. He stopped just before going into the boys' locker room to turn and wave at her.

Angelina was a good two blocks away from the school when Jennifer Hill pulled up beside her in their minivan and Abby slid the back door open.

"Want a ride?" Angelina looked at Abby and smiling through glistening eyes, scrambled into the van. Bobby, who was eleven and Tina, who was eight, Abby's little brother and sister, were bouncing around in the back seats. Abby pulled the door shut and Jennifer took off. "Hi, Angelina, how are you, honey? Abby told me that Bill and Sally are going to adopt you. I think that is so wonderful for you all. We'll have to have a big celebration when everything is final! Bobby! Tina! Stop bouncing around like that. I can't concentrate on driving when you're doing that. Get your seat belts on right now! Angelina, are you excited about the dance tonight? Abby's got one of my mother's old work dresses, those funny looking black stockings, and a pair of her old shoes. We've got a white-haired wig, and I've got some really good makeup so she'll have wrinkles and everything. Bobby! Stop hitting your sister or you won't go trick-or-treating tonight! Abby, I'll drop your stuff off at the Peters after the game. Tony's picking you up, right? Tina! If you don't want your brother to pick on you, I suggest you don't touch him!"

Abby looked at Angelina, holding her hand over her mouth and rolling her eyes. Angelina was laughing softly into her own hand. Abby leaned close to Angelina and whispered, "Sorry I've been such a creep all week. Do you still want me to spend the night?"

"Of course I do! I'm so sorry about Monday. I do have something important I want to tell you, but I can't just yet. Do you trust me, Abby? Can you wait?"

Abby sat for a minute, looking at Angelina. Angelina didn't blink or look away. Finally Abby let out a big sigh and shrugged her shoulders. "OK. OK. I'll wait, but I'm only waiting because you're my 'almost sister' and I love you so much." Angelina laughed and hugged her.

"Moooooom, Abby and Angelina are hugging!" Bobby stuck his tongue out at them.

"Bobby! What did I tell you about sticking out your tongue? Tina, I told you to put your seat belt on! Angelina, is it OK if I don't pull in the driveway? I'm late getting back to the church to pick up Duane. Abby, can't you help me control your brother and sister?" Angelina grinned at Abby as the van came to a sudden stop. She opened the door and jumped out. "Thanks for the ride, Mrs. Hill. See you at the dance Abby."

The door was barely shut before Mrs. Hill took off. Angelina stood watching as the van rounded the corner heading toward the church. She shook her head laughing at the disappearing van; *no wonder Abby loves coming over so much.*

CHAPTER FOURTEEN

A GREAT WIN AND THE DANCE

As Angelina let herself in the back door, Sally poked her head out of the laundry room. "Wild ride home with the Hills again?"

Angelina laughed. "I can't imagine what it must be like living in that house. Do you think it's always that crazy?" Grabbing some grapes out of the bowl on the counter and popping a few into her mouth, she walked down the hall to the laundry room.

Sally was folding jeans and hanging up shirts. Angelina wiped her hands on her pants and started to match up the socks on the countertop as Sally answered her question. "Oh, I don't know. It seems a little wild and crazy to us because we're us and not them. It's probably just a normal day for them." She paused, glancing sideways at Angelina. "So, I guess Abby is still coming to spend the night?"

Angelina carefully matched up a pair of Bill's. "Yeah, she's still coming. Mom, I really need to tell Abby the same as I did Jordan. She knows I'm hiding something and she thinks I don't trust her.

Jordan says we can trust her and I trust his judgment."

Sally folded the last pair of jeans and set them on the stack she had on the counter. She turned, and, folding her arms across her chest, leaned against the counter and stood silently looking at Angelina. Alex came around the corner and rubbed up against Angelina's leg. She bent over and picked him up. Holding him close, she scratched behind his ears. His purring rumbled deep in his chest, and he reached out his paw and patted her cheek. Sally laughed as Angelina asked, "Are you hungry, you handsome fellow? Is your food dish empty? How could that have happened? My goodness, you're going to waste away to nothing!" She cooed to him before putting him down and headed for the kitchen.

Sally sighed, and, picking up the pile of jeans, followed her. As Angelina filled Alex's dish with food and fresh water, Sally headed upstairs to put the jeans away. Angelina followed shortly, going to her own room to change for the game.

She changed quickly out of her slacks and sweater to jeans and a sweatshirt. After pulling on her boots, she went into her bathroom to put her hair up in a ponytail. Sally came in carrying her Tinker Bell costume on a hanger. She hung it on the hook over the closet door and then came to stand in the bathroom doorway. Again, she stood with arms folded, leaning against the doorframe.

"Ok, here's the deal. Your dad and I actually talked about this after you went to bed last night. I'm almost 100% convinced it's OK to tell Abby. He's not but is willing to trust *our* judgment. Just remember, Angelina, she will probably not be too shook up by what you tell her, but she may feel that she can't keep the secret from her parents, and I just don't know how they will handle it. If she thinks she can't keep it from them, well, we can help her forget. She needs to know that too. OK?"

~ CHAPTER FOURTEEN ~

"Ok Mom. Thanks."

Just then Bill blasted the horn of his truck as he pulled into the driveway. Sally turned and headed for the door but stopped to say, "Looks like your dad's home. I think I'll suggest that he buy us hot dogs and other good junk food at the game for supper."

Angelina stepped out of the bathroom and saw the costume hanging on the door of the closet. She hurried over to look at it. "Oh, Mom, this is wonderful!" she exclaimed as she looked closely at the wings. They looked so delicate, but after touching them she could tell they were very sturdy. She turned to Sally, who was still standing at the door, smiling, and hurried over to give her a hug. "Thanks, Mom, for everything! You're the best! That may be a normal day for the Hills, but I'm really, really glad I'm going to belong to you and Dad! I love you guys so much."

Sally hugged her back and then brushed a tear from her eye. "I'm going to go get the rest of the laundry and tell Bill he's taking us to dinner at the game!" She laughed as Angelina clapped her hands and jumped up and down in mock excitement over eating at the game. Her hand reached out and touched a loose curl at the side of Angelina's face. Then she turned and left the room.

Angelina looked at her costume again, then quickly rechecked her hair, grabbed her jacket, and ran down the stairs to the kitchen. Bill stood at the kitchen desk looking over the mail. Sally flipped off the light in the laundry room and headed down the hall toward the kitchen. She paused at the doorway her arms full of laundry still warm from the dryer, its crisp woodsy fragrance filling the room. "I'll be ready in about ten minutes. We'll want to get to the school early for good seats. Are you going to change, Bill?"

Bill dropped the mail. "Yup; race you upstairs!" He was through the kitchen door and halfway up the stairs before Angelina could blink. Sally turned to her and said in a dry tone of voice, "You see what he does when I have my arms full? That's because he knows he doesn't stand a chance otherwise. Sad, isn't it?" Angelina could hear Bill roaring in protest from the top of the stairs. Sally winked at Angelina as she headed for the stairs.

Angelina stood listening to the two of them horsing around above her, laughing and teasing each other. She hugged herself in total happiness. *Please, God, don't let anything happen to keep me from becoming their daughter!*

Angelina nervously watched the scoreboard where the time was ticking away. The clock had been stopped at forty seconds so the Baker's Bluff Indians could take their next to last time-out. After two horrible Fridays of losing, the game had turned into a moment-to-moment breathtaking event.

Bill emptied the last of the popcorn from the bag he was holding into his mouth and turned to Angelina. "They're gonna run it! I just know it! It's a long run, but I think they can pull it off if they set up properly. The Appleton Eagles are a good team, but our guys are better." His voice shook with excitement and emotion. As the huddle broke up and the two teams came together on the line of scrimmage, Bill stood up yelling, "OK, team, show those Eagles that the Indians rule!"

Angelina laughed and looked over at Sally, who winked at her.

Suddenly everyone in the stands was on their feet, yelling and cheering. Greg hesitated before throwing the ball. An Appleton Eagle guard nailed Jason while he was running, looking back for the ball. Greg's head snapped around, and then the ball was flying through the air. Jordan leaped high, caught the ball, and spun away from the one Eagle player who had been guarding him and ran the last forty yards for a touchdown. The cheerleaders went wild on the edge of the field in front of the stands, shouting a cheer that the crowd joined in on. Coach Timson gave the signal for their last time-out.

Angelina looked up at the scoreboard. Home- -22. Eagles- -22, with only fifteen seconds on the clock. Angelina looked at Bill. "I bet they go for the two-point conversion!" he exclaimed, panting for breath.

Angelina watched, holding her breath as the two teams lined up again. The clock started ticking. Greg turned and faked a pass off to Jordan, who turned and started running. Greg then threw the ball to Jason, who caught the ball and stepped back two steps to complete the two-point conversion play. The buzzer screamed the end of the game and the crowd and players went wild. The team members picked up Greg, Jason, and Jordan and carried them off the field. Bill hugged Sally, then Angelina. *"Can you see Jason and Jordan? They're giving each other high fives!"* Bill kissed Angelina on the forehead. *"It's gonna be OK, kiddo!"*

Bill, Sally, and Angelina made their way to the car. It took a good fifteen minutes because of all the people who kept stopping them to congratulate them on the upcoming adoption. Five minutes after they reached the car, Jordan and Jason, along with Austin and Travis, came walking out the side door of the boy's locker room and slowly came down the hill toward the parking lot. Angelina waved at Jordan and he waved back. He turned to Jason, and again, they all gave each other high fives. Jordan then turned toward Angelina while Jason, Austin, and Travis went off in a different direction.

The whole ride back to the house Jordan bubbled over with excitement about the last two plays. Bill kept him talking with his questions and comments about the game. Once they reached the house Jordan said he would be about twenty minutes, since he had to take a quick shower.

Sally helped Angelina put on her costume. Getting her long hair up to put on the shorthaired wig was the biggest challenge. Bill's suggestion to just cut it all off resulted in Sally pushing him out of the room and shutting the door.

When Angelina was finally ready, she came out of her room and started down the stairs. Bill was standing in the entryway with Jordan, who looked up at Angelina. His mouth fell open in amazement. Three-fourths of the way down the stairs, she stepped off the step and hovered in the air, pulling gently on the cord that made the wings flutter. Then, continuing to pull on the cord, she slowly drifted the rest of the way down the stairs.

Evelyn, who had come over with Jordan to take a picture, clapped her hands in childish delight. "Wouldn't you two be the life of the dance if you came in with Angelina fluttering about just over your head?" She laughed with teasing delight at Bill's scowl.

Sally grinned as Bill shook his head, and looked pointedly at Angelina. "No fluttering about at the dance! We don't want mass hysteria on our hands, especially after all the time your mom put in getting the place fixed up so special. Be good, Angelina. OK?"

Angelina's slippers touched down on the floor in front of Bill, and she looked up at him with a pout on her face. "OK, party pooper."

"Aw, come on, Angelina. Promise me you'll be good."

She looked up at Bill with love in her eyes. "I'll be good, Dad, I promise."

After Evelyn and Sally took a few pictures, Bill drove Angelina and Jordan to the school. He spoke confidingly to Jordan when they got out of the car. "You're going to walk the girls home, right?"

~ CHAPTER FOURTEEN ~

"Yes, Mr. Peters, I'll make sure they get home OK." Jordan shut the car door, and he and Angelina headed toward the gym door. *"You can call me Bill, or you can call me Will, or you can call me Phil, but don't ya call me Nil or Till or Lill or...."*

Angelina and Jordan were both laughing as they turned to wave at Bill, who was pulling away with his arm out the window waving.

As they entered the gym, both Jordan and Angelina stopped and gasped with awe. With no outside light coming in from the high windows and only the lighted trees and candles on the tables, the slowly spinning crystal ball gave the room a magical wonderland effect. Angelina whispered, "It's amazing!"

Greg Burns, dressed as Indiana Jones, whip hanging from his belt, and Jill Morton, dressed in an Indiana Jones theme costume, came walking up to them. Greg and Jordan grasped arms. "Good game," they both said at the same time, and then laughed. Greg grinned wickedly. "I like your tights." Jill hit him in the arm, but Jordan just laughed.

Jill looked at Angelina and smiled. "Did Sally make your costume? It's really great. Do those wings move?" Angelina pulled on the cord and the wings fluttered. "That is so way cool!"

As the four of them walked over to get some punch, Jason came in, dressed as Captain Hook, followed by Travis and Austin who were both dressed as pirates. Jason turned just as Amy entered dressed as Wendy. The four of them stood looking around the room for a moment, and then headed for a table not too far from the punch table. Jordan and Jason saw each other and both nodded.

Angelina saw Abby and Tony come in and waved them over. Wendy Greene, whose dad drove the one Baker's Bluff school bus, came in with Ethan Jenks, a lineman on the football team. Both were dressed as characters from Harry Potter. Ethan stopped to talk to Jason, while Wendy hurried over to talk to Jill; both girls were on the cheerleading squad and were excited about the new routine they had performed for the first time earlier at the game.

As the gym continued to fill with students and teachers, Angelina watched Jordan with a feeling of jealous pride. Fellow students kept coming up to him, laughing and talking about the game. Ethan came over to get Wendy, just as Katie Andrews, Marney Burns, and Melissa Doolittle came in dressed as a nurse, a mad scientist, and a waitress. Up on the stage, the students who were playing in the pop band started to warm up. Mr. Campbell walked over to the DJ, picked up a wireless microphone, and walked to the center of the stage.

Mr. Damon, the Band and Orchestra teacher, signaled his son, Dennis who was sitting at the drums, for a drum roll. Denton, his twin brother, joined him with a string of cords on the electric guitar.

Mr. Campbell, standing in the spotlight, raised his hand for silence. "Well, young ladies and gentlemen, it looks like we have a full house of fine and mysterious characters. Let me take a moment first to congratulate our fine team on their spectacular win tonight over the Appleton Eagles." With that the room erupted with thunderous applause, whistling, and cheering. Mr. Campbell raised his hand again, waiting for the noise to die down.

"Before this celebration gets under way, let me remind you that there are teachers here who will, and I stress, will remove anyone found with alcohol in their possession, and there will be unpleasant consequences. There's a wonderful array of food across the hall in the cafeteria; our thanks to all the mothers of the PTA who contributed. As some of you may know, Mr. Jon Guber, is not only a pharmacist, he also happens to be a great freelance photographer and has graciously offered to take pictures, for a small fee, of you kids in your fine duds. And, now, last but not least, it is my pleasure to announce whom you all chose as you king and queen for this great homecoming event."

Miss Annabelle Bruster, Mr. Campbell's secretary, walked across the stage, the clipping of her heels echoing around the now silent gym, with an envelope in her hand. Mr. Campbell took the envelope and ripped it open. "Well, it looks like you decided you wanted Greg Burns as your king and Jill Morton as your queen!"

Again, the room erupted in cheering and applause. Jordan was pounding Greg on his back, and Angelina was hugging Jill as the cheering, whistling, and applause continued. Greg turned to Jill and offered her his arm. The two of them walked to the stage. After both had been crowned, Mr. Campbell again took the microphone. "I present to you, King Greg and Queen Jill. Let the celebration begin!"

Mr. Campbell handed the microphone back to the DJ, who immediately welcomed everyone to a fun-filled musical night of wonder and delight. He said he would be playing a mixture of popular hits, country, and oldies, but would also take requests. The band then started the first song.

Angelina watched as Greg led Jill over to Mr. Guber to get their picture taken. With the starting of the music, couples went out onto the dance floor and started dancing. Jordan reached over and touched her arm. "Want to dance?"

Angelina looked at him and smiled. "Sure."

The first twenty minutes Angelina and Jordan danced just with each other. Then Greg and Jill came over, and Greg twirled Angelina away. Jill took Jordan's hand and led him out onto the floor. "Come on, big boy, relax. She's in safe hands."

Later Abby and Tony separated them again. Tony grinned at Angelina as Abby and Jordan danced off. "Come on Angelina, or should I say, Tinker Bell, let's dance." Angelina laughed as he spun her around.

When the song ended, Jordan and Abby came up to Angelina and Tony. "You want something to eat?" Jordan asked. Standing just inside the door of the gym, the smells from across the hall drifted in, teasing their already growing appetites with anticipation for what they would find. Angelina nodded; taking her arm, Jordan led her across the hall to the cafeteria. The PTA had put forth a gallant effort to provide a wide variety of foods to choose from. There were several different salads and vegetable trays with different types of dips. There were fruit trays with dip, and tortilla chips and salsa. Besides the hot chicken wings, meatballs, and pizza, there was popcorn, caramel apples, and all kinds of desserts. Jordan and Angelina slowly walked the length of the tables, picking and choosing the items that looked good to them. Jordan offered to carry her plate while Angelina picked up two cans of pop for them. Back at their table they sat eating their food and talking to Abby and Tony, who joined them.

When the band started playing a song that Angelina liked, she grabbed Jordan's hand and pulled him to his feet. "Come on, 'Peter', dance with your 'Tinker Bell'." Abby and Tony laughed as they watched them moved out onto the dance floor. Holding Angelina in his arms, Jordan looked into her eyes. *"Are you having a good time?"*

Angelina smiled. *"Yes, very much, you?"*

"When I'm dancing with you I am."

She looked surprised and raised one eyebrow. *"Didn't you have fun dancing with Abby?"*

Jordan grinned. *"Oh, it was OK. Jill wasn't too bad either.*

~ CHAPTER FOURTEEN ~

Ouch! You stepped on my foot on purpose!"

Angelina laughed. *"Oh, sorry. Maybe you won't be able to dance anymore."*

Grinning, he spun her round and round.

As the song ended, Jordan didn't let go but continued to hold Angelina close. She felt a strange, wonderful warmth flowing through her. As the DJ started the next music set, Jordan started them dancing again but stopped at the startled look on Angelina's face.

He turned to see Jason and Amy standing behind him, looking at them. "Can we trade for this dance?" Jason asked haltingly. Amy blushed nervously as Jason held out her hand to Jordan. Jordan didn't move for a moment; then he grinned and, turning to Angelina, winked and placed her hand in Jason's. Taking Amy's hand, Jordan twirled her away, leaving Angelina with Jason.

At first Angelina tensed up when Jason put his hand on her waist, but she finally relaxed. He really was a good dancer. "Those last two plays tonight in the game were great. I couldn't believe it when that line guard tackled you." Angelina could feel how tense Jason was through his hand on her waist. "Bill was so excited! He said you guys would do the two-point conversion over the extra-point play. You guys were awesome tonight. It's great to have both you and Jordan back in the game."

As the song came to an end, Jason stopped dancing and stood looking at her, his blue gray-eyes as troubled as the seashore during a raging storm. "Look," he said, his voice barely audible, "I know you think I'm a jerk most of the time, but Jordan said he was willing to give me a second, third, even a fourth chance, so I hope we can at least be friends." As he turned to walk away, Angelina reached out and caught his arm. "Thank you for the dance, Captain Hook, it was my pleasure to be your partner."

Jason smiled and then turned and walked up to Jordan, who was escorting Amy back to him. The two of them then walked over to Austin and Travis, who were talking to Marney and Melissa.

Jordan walked up to Angelina. "Is everything OK?"

Angelina didn't look at him. She was watching Jason slip his arm around Amy's waist. She sighed and slipped her arm through Jordan's. "Yes, everything is just fine."

CHAPTER FIFTEEN

ABBY LEARNS ABOUT THE SECRET

Jordan and Angelina walked hand in hand beside Abby. They had left the dance at 11:00 to walk home. As they turned the corner onto Center Street, Abby, who had been chattering away about the dance, and Tony, suddenly stopped walking and talking. She watched as Jordan and Angelina slowly approached the driveway to Angelina's house.

"He didn't say anything to me the whole time we danced. I kept talking about the game, and how great it was to have you both back in the game, and he didn't say anything until the dance ended."

"What did he say then?"

"Well, he said: 'Look, I know you think I'm a jerk most of the time, but Jordan said he was willing to give me a second, third, even a fourth chance, so I hope we can at least be friends.' Then he just turned and walked away. What do you think?"

"Well, I think it's a good sign, don't you? I mean, he's kind of holding out the olive branch, don't you think?"

~ ABBY LEARNS ABOUT THE SECRET ~

Sally interrupted their conversation: *"You two are being very rude to Abby!"* Abby had started walking again, kicking at the leaves on the sidewalk.

Angelina caught Abby's thoughts. *"Look at them! Are they so stuck on each other they've forgotten I'm even here? Maybe Angelina would rather I NOT spend the night."*

As Jordan jerked his hand from Angelina's, Angelina turned to look at Abby, who was several yards behind them. Angelina opened her mouth to try and reassure Abby, but no words came out. She turned instead to stare at Jordan as be blurted out in excitement, "I could hear her thoughts! I must be able to hear what you hear when we are touching!"

Abby stopped dead in her tracks, her face almost as white as the wig on her head. Bill and Sally were both coming out the front door and down the steps. *"Abby, Abby, don't be afraid. It's OK. Come into the house, honey."*

Angelina and Jordan each grabbed an arm to help support Abby and helped her into the house. They led her into the family room and the three of them sat down on the couch. Sally came in and held out a mug of hot cider to Abby. "Go ahead, Abby, sip it slowly. It'll help you calm down."

Abby held the mug and then looked at Angelina, who giggled as she said, "Go ahead and drink it. It's not poison or anything."

Bill and Sally sat down across from Abby and waited as she sipped the cider. After Abby set the mug down, she clenched her hands together tightly. Sally smiled kindly at her.

"Abby, can you tell me what have you been thinking and feeling about Angelina lately?"

Abby's deep blue eyes got very large. She looked first at Angelina, and then at Jordan, who nodded encouragingly at her.

~ CHAPTER FIFTEEN ~

"Well, I've known for a long time that there was something different about Angelina. I mean, she kind of has a knack for knowing my moods almost before I know them myself. I've felt at times that Angelina *knew* what I was thinking. And then, there's that weird thing that happened in the pool when she dove in and saved Amy." Abby paused for a moment then went on in a rush, almost defiantly, "And, there's the fact that I can hear YOU, even though you are not talking out loud!"

With shaking hands she reached for the mug of cider and took another sip.

Bill patted Sally's hand and then said, "Abby, I want to reassure you that we are not some weird aliens from outer space. Nor are we evil witches and warlocks, who worship the devil. I'm sure you've heard a little of the history of Baker's Bluff. How back in 1882, Jonathan Baker saw the meteor that fell and formed what is today Baker's Canyon. When that meteor fell, almost one hundred and twenty one years ago, there was no town of Baker's Bluff. There were only scattered settlers in the mountains, about twenty-five families. Jonathan Baker rallied all the men, and they went and checked out the meteor site. It had cleared a wide path of destruction, but it also went deep into the ground, drawing the earth and rocks and trees in with it."

"The area around Henderson Mine Works looks a lot different today than it did that day. Bits and pieces of the meteor had broken off and were scattered all over the ground. Alexander Henderson knew that his land would never be able to be farmed like he had hoped, but Jonathan Baker convinced him that the metal found in the meteor was worth mining, and that's how the mine came to be. Jonathan Baker helped Alexander Henderson get the mine started. Alexander named the mine and Jonathan named the town that sprung up almost overnight."

"It was just a mining town at first, but as the years have gone by, especially the last thirty-five years, the town has grown to what it is today. The mine pretty much played out after about thirty years. Most of the miners and their families who had moved here to work in the mine moved on once the mine slowed down. Some stayed, and of the original twenty-five families, some of them have stayed down through the generations. Those who stayed, well, it wasn't long before they started noticing that they could do strange things. You know Old Doc Adams, don't you?"

Abby nodded.

"Well, let me give you a little background. Albert Adams was twenty-one years old in 1882 when the meteor fell. His son Daniel was born seven years later in 1889. Daniel completed medical school training the year his son Philip was born, in 1913. That was the year the mine cut way back in its mining production. A lot of the mining folks left Baker's Bluff that year. Daniel took blood samples from a lot of the 'old' original settlers who were still around, and samples from members of their families. He was very curious to know if there was something in the blood that made them different."

"The study of cells and the genetic code was just getting started when Daniel took the blood samples. He didn't have the equipment or means to really study the samples he took, but he was careful and preserved the slides for future study."

"Dr. Joseph Adams, Philip's son, was born in 1939; following in his grandfather Daniel's footsteps, he completed medical school in 1967. His recent studies of the slides his grandfather had made show, with all the updated equipment and tests, an extremely high level of ATP's in the blood cells. EEGs done very recently show that we use 70% more of our brain than other people do. In general, our brains are 75% more active than other people."

"The bottom line is that something changed in our cells' molecular structure and our genetic code. More areas of our brain are active, and as a whole, our brains are just plain more active. At this point in time, our best guess for why we can do what we do is that something related to that meteor falling changed our ancestors and was genetically passed on down to us."

Abby was now sitting on the edge of the couch, listening intently to Bill. "What kind of strange things did they notice they could do?" she asked in a hushed voice, her curiosity piqued beyond the borders of her fear of the unknown.

"I guess I should have said special abilities rather than strange things. Anyway, let's see. Well, for one thing they could hear other people's thoughts. They could communicate with each other telepathically. They were able to move things without touching them, telekinetically. And they could move themselves..." Bill stopped talking because Abby was startled when she suddenly became aware of Angelina floating in the air above her head.

As Abby caught her breath, Jordan put his arm around her, and laughed. "Listen, Abby, she's just showing off. Bill told her she was not to 'flutter' about like Tinker Bell, and ever since, she's been dying to do it."

"Angelina, behave." Bill's voice sounded stern, but he winked at Abby. Slowly Angelina settled back down on the couch beside Abby.

Sally reached over and took Abby's hand in hers. "There's nothing to be afraid of, Abby. Believe me."

"I've told you all of this, Abby," Bill continued, "so you would understand what I have to tell you next. Exposure to the meteor did not affect everyone. The new little town went through some hard times. Whenever someone would use their special abilities around someone who didn't have the abilities, well it was cause for fear and suspicion, and yes, jealousy. Some people thought that the people who had these special abilities were evil. Some people were hurt, and some even died."

Bill paused for a moment and then asked, "Abby, do you understand why we have to ask you not to share our secret with anyone?"

Abby was no longer looking at Bill but was staring, at Sally, who was still holding her hands. Abby slowly nodded her head, an amazed, faraway look in her eyes.

Bill pressed further. "Do you think you can keep our secret?"

Sally gently patted Abby's hands before she released them. Abby swallowed hard and then looked at Bill and said yes.

Bill looked at her quietly for a moment then added, "You know, Abby, it's OK if you can't keep our secret. We'll understand, and we won't be mad at you. We can even help you forget everything you have seen and heard tonight if that would be better for you."

Abby's eyes became very large with alarm and she jumped up. "NO! I don't want to forget. PLEASE!" She turned to Jordan. "How long have you known all of this?"

Jordan grinned sheepishly. "For sure, just since the night in the hospital after the fight on the football field."

"You're OK with this?" Her eyes searched his face for the truth.

Jordan didn't blink as he answered firmly. "Yes."

Abby turned to look at Angelina and smiled. "Then I am too, my 'almost sister'. I am too." Angelina and Abby hugged each other.

Jordan heaved a big sigh, and smiled at Bill as he slowly stood up. "I better get home. I have detention again tomorrow morning."

Bill walked Jordan to the door. When they reached the front door Bill said, "Don't worry Jordan. You didn't cause any trouble tonight. We were going to tell Abby anyway. You just kind of got the ball rolling for us."

Angelina came running out of the family room. "See you tomorrow after detention, OK?"

Jordan nodded. "See you tomorrow, Angelina. I had a great time tonight."

As Bill closed the front door, Angelina and Abby headed for the stairs to go up to Angelina's room. Sally came out into the entryway. "Good night, girls."

Abby paused at the bottom of the stairs to pick up the overnight bag her mom had dropped off after the game, but Angelina grabbed it, so she turned to Bill and Sally. "Good night, Mr. and Mrs. Peters. Thanks for trusting me enough to tell me all of this."

When Abby looked back at Angelina, she was shocked to discover Angelina was already at the top of the stairs looking down at her.

Now she's really showing off. Abby looked back at Sally and blinked in surprise from hearing her speak in her mind, and just as suddenly found herself beside Angelina at the top of the stairs. As Abby let out a startled squeak, Angelina laughed. "Now who's showing off?"

Angelina shut her bedroom door and dropped Abby's bag on the bed. Abby flopped down on the bed. "Holy cow! So is all of this what you needed to work out before you could tell me? Did you know that I could see things when Bill was telling me why it was so important that I keep this a secret? I could see the things that happened to those people! So, how did I get up the stairs? Did you do that? What else can you do?"

Angelina sighed. *It's going to be a long night.*

CHAPTER SIXTEEN

THIRD DETENTION AND WHAT FOLLOWED

Jason was already at his desk the next morning when Jordan walked into Mr. Allen's classroom. Austin and Travis had not arrived yet. Jason did not look up or acknowledge Jordan when he slipped into his seat. Five minutes later, when Travis and Austin arrived, Jason did look up at them, and for a split second Jordan could see the bruises on the side of his face. *Now what happened?*

Mr. Allen walked over to the chalkboard and wrote out the assignment:

1. List the current types of relationships that you have.
2. List who the relationships are with.
3. Rate how important the relationships are.

When Mr. Allen had written out the assignment, he turned to the boys. "I'll give you twenty minutes to make your lists, and then we'll have a discussion about them." Without another word he walked back over to his desk, sat down, picked up the book he had been reading, and seemed to totally ignore the boys.

Jordan sighed as he picked up his pencil to start on his list. He glanced over at Jason, who was still staring at the board. Austin and Travis were writing, laughing and snickering, hiding what they were writing from each other. Jason slowly picked up his pencil and started to write.

Twenty minutes later Mr. Allen closed his book, stood up, and asked for a volunteer to read his list.

Travis raised his hand. "I'll go first. I might as well get this over with." He stood up and cleared his throat. "OK, first I have a parent/child relationship with my parents, William and Elizabeth. I would have to say it's an important relationship. I need to stay on their good side. The allowance thing, ya know?" He chuckled self-consciously and then continued. "Then there's the sibling relationship with my twin sister, Katie. That's an important one too. I need to stay on her good side too. We live in the same house and share a bathroom. If she wanted to she could make my life a living nightmare." He paused for a moment as Austin snorted with laughter.

"Then there are my buddies, Jason and Austin. My relationship with them is VERY important. I mean, come on, we watch each other's back." He turned to Austin and they gave each other a high five.

"Then there is that most amazing teacher/student relationship. I guess I would have to say the relationships between my teachers and me are important by necessity. I need good grades to pass, and I need to pass to graduate, and I need to graduate to go to college or get a good job. It's a vicious circle."

He paused to glance over at Mr. Allen whose face hadn't changed despite the snickers from Austin and Jason. Quickly he continued. "Oh, and I guess I also have relationships between my classmates and friends and myself. Like Melissa Doolittle, for instance; she's kinda cute, though I don't think she knows I exist. Anyway, I think it's important to have friends. They keep life from getting dull."

Travis folded his paper and sat down as Jason and Austin clapped. "Thank you, Travis. That was very interesting. Looks like all your relationships are important to you. That's good. So, who wants to go next?" Mr. Allen waited patiently for one of the other three to get up.

Jason pushed his chair out roughly and stood up. "I'll go next. I think that the parent/child relationship is the most important one for me, especially the one with my mom, Ann. She really cares about us. She's kind of the glue that holds us together as a family. Now my dad, George, well all he really cares about is the gas station. I don't think he would care if I disappeared, except that he needs me to help out at the station." Jason could not hide the bitterness in his voice. Even his laugh sounded bitter as he added, "Oh, yeah, football is important to him too. Win or lose, I could always have done better."

"Then of course there's my sister, Jill, filling the bill for the 'sibling' relationship. I guess my relationship with her is important too, because, well if something happened to Mom, all we'd have is each other, because Dad sure wouldn't be there for us." Again the bitterness Jason so keenly felt could be heard in his every word and could be seen in the tortured look in his eyes. He cleared his throat and continued.

"And, my buddies, Travis and Austin, yeah, they're important to me. It's like Travis said, we watch each other's backs." Jason glanced at Mr. Allen before continuing. "Teacher/student relationships are important too. I need to graduate so I can get out of here." Jason paused again, shuffling his paper in his hand. Then he looked at Jordan. "Friendships with classmates are a type of relationship I'm not all that familiar with. I guess I'm still trying to figure that one out."

Jason sat down without looking at Travis and Austin who started to clap. Mr. Allen raised his hand for silence. He looked thoughtfully at Jason. "That was very interesting, Jason, and honest. There will be times in our life when we have relationships that will be difficult, challenging, disturbing, confusing, and hopefully, rewarding. Acknowledging them for what they are is not a sign of weakness or failure. It's actually a sign of maturity. Each relationship is a learning experience. What we do with that learning experience, well, that's the real kicker. OK, who's next?"

Jordan slowly stood up, holding his sheets of paper in his hand. "I guess I feel the same as Jason and Travis, in that I think the parent/child relationship is important enough to mention it first. The relationship I have with my mom, Evelyn, is VERY important to me. She's all I have, and I'm all she has since my dad walked out on us." Jordan knew his own words had a ring of bitterness to them, but he pushed quickly on.

"I also have a good relationship with my neighbors, Bill and Sally Peters. They've been like family, not only to me, but to my mom too. They care a lot about us. They've really been there for us, and their friendship means a lot to me."

Jordan focused hard on his paper, making it a point not to look at Mr. Allen. "I have to agree that the relationship between students and teachers is very important. I only have a student's perspective, but I really think that how well a student learns and applies what he learns depends a lot on the relationship he has with the teacher. I don't mean doing what you have to do to get the teacher to pass you. I mean an open and honest relationship where you can interact with that teacher and not feel stupid or put down. A great teacher knows this and is able to develop that kind of relationship or atmosphere, and then I think learning just happens. A great teacher will help a student to keep on track with his studies so he can go to college or a trade school or whatever." Austin snickered but suddenly gasped when Jason kicked him in the shins.

"I think I get along with most of my classmates, but I do think that friendships are very important, kind of like a support system." He paused to glance at Jason, who was now staring at him with a look Jordan could not read. He pushed on. "A true friend will always tell you the truth, even if you don't want to hear it. They will listen, and not judge you, and they will stand by you through the good times and the bad. They laugh with you in the good, funny times, and they stand by your side, ready to hold you up in the bad, the sad times. And they don't laugh at you if you cry."

Jordan felt his face flush as he continued. "It's funny, until a couple of weeks ago, I hadn't really thought much about a 'girl-friend' relationship. Angelina Beacon has been a part of my life since shortly after I moved here with my parents. We've lived next door to each other for over six years now. I guess I thought she would always be there. Lately I've come to realize that she does all the things a true friend does, and next to my mom, she is the most important person in my life." Jordan paused and looked up at Mr. Allen, surprise and wonder on his face. "And ya know, I haven't even told her that." Jordan suddenly felt very awkward and quickly stared down at his paper for a minute. "I guess that's it." He sat down, folded up his papers, and stuffed them in the back pocket of his pants.

Mr. Allen cleared his throat. "That was thought-provoking, Jordan. It is important to understand the different relationships that we have. Each one is unique. Each one is important, in different ways.

Well, Austin, it looks like it's your turn."

Austin stood up, clearing his throat. "Yeah, I guess it's my turn. I guess I'm a little like Jordan, in that I only have one parent. It's just my dad- -Jonathan- -and me. We only have each other since my mom died last year. I miss Mom a lot; she took real good care of Dad and me. My dad, he's still having a real hard time of it. Anyway..."

Austin coughed, trying to clear his throat. "The teacher/student thing is important, because I need to graduate. And my buds, Travis and Jason, they're really important to me. Like they said, we watch each other's back."

Austin paused for a moment, and suddenly his face blushed deep red. "Friendships with my classmates, hmm? Well, I guess I don't have very many tight ones except Jason and Travis. I guess I get along with most everybody though. I do kinda like Marney Burns, but she's way too smart for me." Austin looked over at Mr. Allen with alarm. "What we say here stays here, right, Mr. Allen?"

Mr. Allen came around the front of his desk and sat on the edge. "Yes, what we say in this room, in my car, or out on my farm, doesn't go any further. Does every one understand that?" Each boy nodded.

"OK, let's review the relationships we've discussed." Mr. Allen walked to the blackboard and wrote:

1. Parent / Child
2. Sibling
3. Buddies
4. Teacher / Student
5. Classmates/friends
6. Neighbors
7. Girlfriend

"Can any of you think of other types of relationships not mentioned?" As each of the boys took turns firing out other types of relationships, Mr. Allen wrote them on the board.

8. Law enforcement / Public
9. Preacher / Congregation

10. Doctor / Patient
11. Pet / Owner
12. Different family members: Aunts, Uncles, Cousins, Grandparents
13. Employer / Employee

Mr. Allen held up his hand and turned to face the boys. "OK, what are some of the things that can fuel a relationship?" Again the boys started firing out answers that Mr. Allen wrote in another column.

1. Anger
2. Sadness
3. Loneliness
4. Hate
5. Love
6. Insecurity
7. Happiness
8. Excitement
9. Resentment
10. Contentment
11. Bitterness
12. Disappointment

Again, Mr. Allen stopped them. "I think you've given me a pretty good list. Your assignment for our last detention next Friday after the game will be to write out in essay format how these things affect the relationships in our life. Be sure to bring your completed assignment with you next Friday. Now, when we get out to my house today we will examine the map I have of the area we will be hiking to next Friday, and we will be practicing some climbing techniques."

Jordan scribbled down on the back of his paper the list Mr. Allen had made and then put his jacket on to head out to the Land Rover.

As he approached the Land Rover, he heard Austin say to Travis. "This detention hasn't been so bad, but I'll be glad when it's over so things can get back to normal."

Jordan stopped walking, deeply shaken by what he had just overheard. He looked over at Jason, who was leaning up against the

Land Rover waiting for Mr. Allen to come out of the school. Jason was looking at him with a guarded look. Jordan sighed in resignation and sadly shook his head. *Maybe this isn't really working after all.*

It was a beautiful fall Sunday afternoon. Angelina and Jordan had decided to go for a ride on the Baker's Bluff bike trail. As she turned her bike off the street onto the marked bicycle trail she began peddling hard, trying to catch up with Jordan. He had come home from detention on Saturday in a bad mood. She knew how worried he was that Jason had been putting on an act the whole time, and he was concerned that as soon as the detention classes were over he would go right back to acting the way he had before. Jordan was angry and hurt. He had even lashed out at her Saturday night when they went for a walk.

"What a big waste of time! I feel like I've been played for a fool! All this time I thought Jason was serious, was trying to change. It seemed like he was changing. It really did. I feel like such a fool!" Jordan had angrily kicked at the leaves. He had then turned to Angelina, his face a mixture of frustration, anger and hurtful pain. "You know what the worst of it is?" His voice had then broken, and tears had streamed unchecked down his cheeks. "I was starting to like Jason! I was beginning to think that maybe, just maybe, we could be friends. Ya know? Real friends! Stand by your side; tell you the truth kind of friends. Yeah, right!"

Jordan had then turned and had taken off running down the street. Angelina had not followed. She had walked home alone. Sally and Bill had been waiting for her on the porch. *"He just needs a little time alone, honey. Don't worry. It's gonna be OK."*

Angelina stopped peddling and watched as Jordan disappeared around a turn in the trail. She closed her eyes tight, picturing the trail a good hundred yards ahead of where Jordan was.

~ CHAPTER SIXTEEN ~

When she opened her eyes she turned to look behind her to see Jordan peddling hard around the curve in the trail. Spotting her standing in the middle of the trail with her bike, Jordan screeched to a halt. Panting hard to catch his breath, he asked. "How did you get here?"

"Jordan, we're supposed to be having fun! Can't you forget about this thing with Jason for a little while? Worrying about it and being mad isn't going to make things any better."

Jordan walked up to her pushing his bike, his grip on the handlebars so tight his knuckles were turning white. "I can't help it! I feel like this whole thing has been a big waste of time!" Angelina could hear the mounting anger and frustration in his voice.

Reaching down, she calmly flicked a small twig off her jeans, trying not to become upset herself. "Well, if you really believe that all of this has been a big waste of *your* time, and you continue to *act* on that belief, then it *will* have been all for nothing."

As they stood, eyes locked, she could feel his anger about to explode. "What do you want from me?" he yelled. Suddenly he jerked his bike around and headed into the woods, off the trail, not looking where he was going.

Angelina dropped her bike and started running after him. Up ahead of her, Jordan's bike hit a large rock covered with leaves and he went flying over the handlebars. She stared hard at him, and he gently landed on the ground. Instantly she was beside him. "Are you OK?" she asked anxiously.

Jordan sat up slowly with her help and began to brush dirt, leaves and twigs off his shirt and jeans. "Yeah, I guess so, no broken bones, just a wounded pride."

She brushed leaves off his back and then grabbed his hands and pulled him to his feet. "I'm sorry if what I said was out of line and upset you."

He bent over and brushed the last of the leaves off his jeans. "No, you're right; I need to keep believing the best. It's just hard, ya know?"

She reached out and touched his arm. "I am sorry, Jordan. I was just trying to help, but maybe I'm just making things worse."

He sighed and caught her hand. "No, Angelina, you are not making things worse. I need you to keep reminding me, to keep me on track."

His smile changed to a frown as he turned and saw his bike lying on its side with the front wheel bent. "Great! My wheel's bent. Guess I'll be walking back." Kicking at the leaves, he started to walk back to his bike.

Angelina glanced around to see if there was any one else close by. They were a good ten feet off the bike trail and she couldn't *hear* anyone, so she turned her attention to the bike wheel. Very slowly the wheel straightened out.

Jordan reached out a shaking hand and touched the wheel. He turned to look at Angelina. "Wow! You are *REALLY* something!"

Back out on the bike trail, Angelina picked up her bike, and they continued riding, now side by side. The sunlight filtered down through the trees, and the few trees with leaves still on them were bright splashes of color against the deep green of the evergreens. Every now and then birds would flutter across the trail, or a squirrel would scurry up a tree, chattering at them from a safe distance. Once, a hawk soared in a large, lazy circle over their heads. The soft gentle breeze wasn't too cold, so it made for a perfect Indian summer day. It was hard to believe that Thanksgiving was less than four weeks away.

Jordan looked over at Angelina. "Are you getting anxious

about Tuesday's appointment with the attorney?"

She laughed as two squirrels darted across their path and up a tree. With large puffy tails snapping, they chattered loudly as Jordan and Angelina rode under the branch they were perched on. "Sounds like they're scolding us, doesn't it?" She looked at Jordan and smiled. "Yeah, I guess I am a little anxious about the whole thing. But I'm trying not to think about it."

Jordan jerked hard on his handlebars and rode on his back wheel with the front wheel spinning in the air. "So what are you most concerned about?" He let his front wheel bounce back down on the ground and turned to look at Angelina, grinning like a little kid as she rolled her eyes and shook her head.

She laughed as he skidded sideways and struggled to recover his balance. "How much time do you have?" she asked, and then added thoughtfully, "Actually this whole thing has really got me thinking. I've been trying to remember, to see if I have any memories of grandparents, a father, aunts, uncles, or cousins. I can only remember snatches of images from where I lived with my mother before she was killed in a car accident. I was five at the time."

Angelina peddled for a moment, and then went on. "I have some vague images of a very drab brick building. I think it was an apartment building. I remember a woman across the hall with lots of kids, and a little dog that barked a lot. I remember a kind of fat man; his T-shirts were so short, they didn't cover his belly. I remember him on his knees doing something under the sink in the kitchen. He may have been the landlord. I remember standing in a crib; my teddy bear was on the floor. I couldn't reach him. I remember holding out my hands to him and he just floated through the air to me." She glanced at Jordan, who was still riding beside her, staring straight ahead.

Angelina swallowed hard; she'd never told this to anyone

before, except Sally and Bill. She continued, "I remember another time wanting some cookies that were on a plate in the center of the table and reaching out to take one that floated off the table to me. My clearest and last memory of my mother is when we were in the grocery store. I was sitting in the seat of the shopping cart that my mother was pushing. She wasn't putting the potato chips that I wanted in the cart. She said something about not having enough money. So, I thought them to the cart. Mom turned in time to see the chips floating in the air. She said: '*NO! Angelina! Don't ever do that again!*'

"She didn't say the words out loud, but that didn't surprise me. I can remember talking a lot with my mom without talking out loud. I now know that she did not say no to me for taking the chips when she said that we did not have enough money. She said 'NO' because I 'thought' the chips to the cart. But she never got the chance to explain.

"That was the day the accident happened on the way home. Mom '*lifted*' me through the window of the car just before the truck hit us. Everyone who saw the accident swore that I had been thrown from the car by the impact. I mean, what other explanation was there? It was a miracle that I was unharmed. They took Mom away that day under a white sheet. I remember a policeman holding me while I cried."

Angelina and Jordan both stopped riding at the same time. Angelina was shaking hard and began taking slow deep breaths to try to calm down. Jordan put his bike on its kickstand; walking around her bike, he took it from her, setting it on its kickstand. Then he turned and took hold of both of her arms just below her shoulders. "Look at me, Angelina. I'm really sorry about your mom dying and all that you've had to go through. But you have to remember how lucky you are that Bill and Sally found you. I don't think for a minute that it was pure luck that you landed with them and not some other foster home. They really love you, Angelina. And don't you think that way back when all that stuff happened the police didn't check everything out before putting you in the hands of a social worker to be put in foster homes?"

She looked at him through tear-filled eyes. "But what if she was hiding from someone, Jordan?"

He let go of one of her arms and took hold of her chin so she could not look away from him. "Listen to me, you sweet silly worry wart, I just told you that Bill and Sally *REALLY* love you. They are NOT going to let anything bad happen to you, and neither will I!"

Later that evening lying in bed, Angelina remembered how Jordan had given her a big hug after his pep talk and how relaxed she had felt the rest of their ride. They had laughed and talked about the dance and the game all the way home. But now, lying in the dark, she again felt the grip of her fears. Turning on her side she cried softly into her pillow.

Suddenly her door opened and Bill and Sally came in. They both sat down on opposite sides of the bed. Sally reached out and brushed her hair back away from her face. "*Come on, Angelina. Don't cry. Everything is going to work out. You'll see.*"

Angelina turned over and sat up. "Do you know what happened with Jordan and me today?"

Bill looked at her and nodded. "Yes, honey. We heard it all."

Sally turned so she was sitting with her back to Angelina's pillow and put her arm around her. "Angelina, we've been in touch with the attorney. He hasn't come up with any good leads to relatives. Let's not worry about it. Do you believe what Jordan said? That we love you very much and will not let anything bad happen?"

Angelina put her head on Sally's shoulder. "Yes, Mom, I do. I love you both so much!" She put her arms around Sally and rested her head on her chest and continued to cry softly. Sally looked at Bill and nodded.

Bill got up and walked out of the room, gently closing the door behind him. He stood outside the door listening to Sally quietly soothe Angelina. He turned and headed for their room, knowing Sally would not leave till Angelina had fallen asleep.

CHAPTER SEVENTEEN

JASON AND JORDAN'S ESSAYS

When Jordan and Angelina walked into fourth period Creative Writing on Tuesday, the entire class was already there except for them. The only two empty seats left were between Jason and Abby. Angelina took the seat next to Abby and Jordan slipped into the seat next to Jason. Jordan cautiously glanced over at Jason, but he had turned and was leaning over talking to Amy, Travis, and Austin.

Angelina touched his arm. He met her eyes and was touched by the warm, encouraging smile she gave him. She leaned over and whispered, "You remember that I'm leaving right after class? Sally's coming to pick me up and we're going to meet Bill at the attorney's office."

Jordan nodded and smiled back at her, the pressure of her hand still on his arm reassuring. Abby reached over and touched Angelina's arm. *"Everything's going to be OK, Angelina."* Abby leaned to look past Angelina at Jordan. *"That goes for you to Jordan."* Jordan grinned as they all sat back in their seats when the bell rang.

Miss Fisher asked everyone to face the front of the class.

She stood in front of her desk waiting for everyone to quiet down. "I have read all your essay assignments from last week. For the most part, everyone did an exceptional job." She paused as an undercurrent of comments swirled around the room. Miss Fisher cleared her throat. "There were two papers that I felt were outstanding."

She waited for everyone to give her his or her undivided attention. She turned and picked up two writing assignments off her desk. "I am very pleased to say that the two outstanding papers were: Me, Myself written by Jason Morton and If written by Jordan Bradford."

The class erupted with clapping and cheering. Austin and Travis whistled loudly. Jordan and Jason turned to look at each other, shock written all over their faces.

Miss Fisher rapped on her desk to bring the class to order. She turned and smiled proudly at both boys. "These papers were wonderful, and I would like you to take turns and read them aloud to the class."

Jordan and Jason continued staring at each other. Jason was laughing with excited pleasure. Jordan raised his eyebrows, and Jason nodded at him. Winking back at him, Jordan stood up. Jason grinned and gave him a thumb up sign.

Jordan walked to the front of the class, took the sheets of paper that Miss Fisher held out to him, and clearing his throat, began to read:

"No one can really say for sure just how they will react to a situation or event that happens to them. You can make a guess as to how you might react, what you might think, or feel, but you can't really know for sure until it happens. Then, of course, there are other things to think about. Like the age of who's involved, the time leading up to what is happening, the histories of who's involved, the actual situation, and maybe most important of all, the circumstances surrounding the situation.

"The fact is, a guess is simply 'a guess', which can make you wonder about the whole idea of 'if.' But, if you don't have some kind of plan, you can be setting yourself up for a really messy surprise. The surprise alone can throw you such a curve that how you end up actually handling the situation could be totally different from how you might have handled it had you been a little more prepared.

Being prepared doesn't mean you have to do something a certain way. You always have the choice: to do something the way you would because of having thought it through before hand, or you can chose to do something completely different. Whatever the thing is that you are going through, well, that's the real thing. Whatever choice you make, the outcome will start a whole new and different thing, with another choice to make. If you think about all the possible outcomes and all the different 'ifs', well, you could end up in a padded room with no windows.

Here's something to think about. Maybe 'if' you fine yourself facing something, maybe the best thing to do is to take a moment right then to just step back. Take a breather. Give yourself the chance to figure out what you are feeling. Think about whom it is you dealing with? How has this person affected your life - - now, and prior to what's happening right at the moment? Maybe most important is the fact that nothing you go through can be completely devastating if trust and honesty are involved.

"So, what is my 'if'?

"Well, my 'if' is: 'What if I should see my dad again?' What would I say to him? What would he say to me? How would I feel? What would I do? What if he didn't want to talk to me? Would I believe anything he said if he did want to talk to me? Would I even listen to him if he would talk to me? (Remember the padded room?)"

Jordan paused for a moment and glanced at Jason. He swallowed hard trying to keep his composure.

"Like I said, no one knows for sure how they will react to everything they go through. Oh sure, I can guess how I might respond, think, or feel, but I won't know for sure until it happens. And 'if' it happens, well, it's been five years since I last saw my dad. He just might have something to say that I need to hear, and I'm sure I'll have something to say that I want him to hear. So, if. . . ."

Jordan handed the papers back to Miss Fisher and returned

to his seat as the class clapped and cheered. Miss Fisher set the papers down on the desk and was still clapping and smiling at him when he looked up at her. Jordan looked over at Jason, who was clapping and smiling. Even Travis and Austin were clapping and nodding their heads. Jordan saw that Angelina was fighting back tears.

Miss Fisher rapped her desk again with her ruler and asked Jason to stand and read his paper.

Jason walked to Miss Fisher and took the sheets of paper that she handed him. He looked at the papers for a moment, and then glanced at Jordan. Jordan smiled and gave him an encouraging nod.

Jason lifted his head and began with a clear strong voice:

"There are some age-old questions that everyone has asked at some point or time in their life. Who am I? Why am I here? What is the purpose of my life? What makes me the way I am? The search for the answers to those questions has driven many to the very edge of sanity. They have stood gazing into a darkness that is filled with fear, frustration, wonder, and awe; overwhelmed by questions of self-doubt, insecurity, anger, and pain.

"Many, unable to find the answers have plunged head first into that darkness; plummeting into the depths of insanity, into horrific acts of violence, into empty lives. Lives filled with shattered dreams, broken promises, and wasted unfulfilled years. Others, searching for those same answers, have entered into a lifelong quest of wonder and adventure; questioning, testing, learning, and thriving in the ever-changing challenges of life.

"What makes one person teeter over that edge into the darkness, and another jump into life's challenges? Maybe it's a predestined character trait, due to genetics. Maybe it has something to do with upbringing, family relationships. We've all heard those comments: 'You are the spitting image of your daddy,' or 'You have your mamma's eyes.' How about, 'You sound just like your father when you say that.' or 'You are reacting just like your mother!'

"I used to think I was who I was because of my parents. Like, I have red hair because my mom does. I'm tall and muscular because my dad is a big man. I'm left-handed because my dad is. I've got a quick, hot temper because my dad does. My sister says I have such a big mouth because I keep putting my foot in it. (Jason paused and looked up as the class chuckled. He glanced at Jordan, who nodded again encouragingly.)

"The last few weeks I've had some time to think about some of those questions. Things have happened to me that made me . . . No, that's not what I meant to say. I have made some choices and now I am paying for them. If I'm going to be completely honest with myself, then I have to say that I know that I am who I am because of the choices I have made. My so-called reason for why I made the choices really doesn't matter. I am still the one who made them. That's not an easy thing to face up to and admit. (Jason paused to look up at his classmates, and then added a comment softly to the essay:) Especially to a room full of your classmates! But, I'm not going to be 16 and in the 10th grade forever. I've seen the edge of the darkness, and like everyone else, I know frustration and self-doubt. Blaming everything and everyone else hasn't seemed to change anything, at least not for the better. I've been watching someone else these last few weeks that is going through a similar tough time, and I've seen a strength of character that I want. (Jordan stared wide-eyed at Jason as he paused again.)

"So, who am I, really? Why, I'm me, myself."

As Jason laid his papers down on Miss Fisher's desk the class erupted with clapping and cheering. Travis and Austin were whistling. Jason looked at Jordan as he walked back to his desk. Jordan was staring at him with amazement and wonder on his face. Suddenly Jordan let out a shout of delight and jumped up, thrusting out his hand at Jason for a high five. Jason smiled and gave him a high five.

The clapping and cheering continued past the ringing of the bell. As Angelina started packing up her things to leave, she thought to Sally and Bill, *"You are NOT going to believe what just happened!"*

"Oh yes we are, we heard it all!"

Jordan turned and looked at Angelina. *"Hope! It is an awesome thing!"*

CHAPTER EIGHTEEN

APPOINTMENT WITH ATTORNEY JOE ARMSTRONG

Sally and Angelina met Bill at Conner's Pizza Parlor. Conner's Pizza Parlor was a busy popular place to eat in Baker's Bluff. The nostalgic round tables had red and white-checkered tablecloths on them, and the floor was black and white square tile. A large ceiling fan whined as it turned slowly, swirling the aroma of warm pizza dough, garlic, and tomato around the room. The old-fashioned jukebox in the corner was playing an old 50's tune. Amos Conner had opened for business four years earlier. His hopes of establishing a competitive pizza joint were very successful as the place was always busy.

Finding an empty table in the corner, they all tried to relax and eat some pizza before going to their appointment at 1:00 pm with Attorney Joe Armstrong. They discussed Jason and Jordan's essay papers.

Sally took a sip of her pop and smiled at Angelina. "You can sure see that Jordan has his mother's talent for expressing himself on paper. You know, Evelyn finally showed me her manuscript. I read the first six chapters. She's really good!"

Angelina caught a mushroom with her tongue as it slid off the piece of pizza she held in her hand. "Yeah, I know. She's been letting Jordan read each chapter as she finishes it. He said the other day that every time he finishes a chapter he can hardly wait for her to give him the next one. He thinks she's going to be really famous someday." She took a bite of the pizza and continued with her mouth full. "Of course, he can't wait for that! I thought maybe it was because they would then have a little more money. But that's not it at all." She swallowed and set her pizza down, her face registering her concern.

Bill reached out his hand and touched her. She looked up into his kind caring eyes. "It's because he wants to rub it in his dad's face, right?" Angelina nodded sadly.

Bill was thoughtful for a moment, and then asked, "Was that before he wrote his essay?"

Angelina suddenly brightened up. "Yes! Yes it was. I bet that part isn't as important anymore, don't you? I mean, if he really meant what he wrote, it sounds like he's really getting a handle on things, don't you think?"

Sally smiled. "I think he's going to be just fine. Now, you two better finish so we can get to the appointment on time."

Right at one o'clock the three of them walked into the small but neatly furnished office of Joe Armstrong, Attorney at Law. Jessica, Joe's wife, told them he would be with them in just a moment, and offered them coffee or pop. Bill declined for all of them as they had just finished lunch. The small lobby was empty, so Bill and Sally took a seat on the couch while Angelina took a chair across from them.

~APPOINTMENT WITH ATTORNEY JOE ARMSTRONG~

The coarse tweed fabric of the chair gave Angelina's nervous fingers something to pick at. Her nervous fidgeting shifted to nervous action, and she got up to look out the window. After just a few moments she sat down again, only to get back up and walk to the drinking fountain. Back at her chair, she nervously tapped the floor with her foot. Bill and Sally waited patiently, smiling at her sympathetically when she stood up for the third time. She walked over to the rack of magazines and tried to pick out one that looked interesting.

At 1:15 Joe came out of his office, apologizing for making them wait and told Jessica to hold his calls. When they entered his office he motioned them over to a small round table that held three stacks of papers. Several green plants graced the windowsill that looked out on the street. Blinds covered the windows and were at a slant that allowed light but still offered privacy. As they settled in the wood chairs around the marble-topped table, Joe opened a file he had carried with him to the table, pulled out a certificate, and handed it to Angelina.

"This is your birth certificate. I found it in the registrar's office at the county courthouse in Appleton. It has your birth date listed as November 24, 1987. You were born at 1:30 in the morning at Appleton University Hospital. You can see where the father's name should be; it's been left blank. It has your mother's name listed as Elizabeth Beacon. I didn't find any record of a marriage license listed under that name, but that doesn't mean your mom wasn't married. She could have been married anywhere and then came to Appleton to have you."

Angelina sat staring at her birth certificate, goose bumps forming on her arms. Sally slipped her arm around Angelina, who was trembling from the news she had just received. *"Was I illegitimate?"* She was fighting back tears as Sally gave her a reassuring squeeze. *"I don't believe you were, but even if that was true, do you think it really matters?"*

She looked at Sally and smiled, shaking her head no. She caught Bill's quick, *"We love you kiddo!"* and turned her attention back to Mr. Armstrong.

Mr. Armstrong pulled out a legal pad and referred to it for a moment before continuing. "My private investigator did find an old neighbor of Elizabeth's. I believe she lived in the same apartment building that you and your mother lived in. This woman told my man that your mother had told her once that her grandparents had raised her. That they lived in a cabin up in the mountains around Baker's Bluff and that they supposedly died in a fire before Angelina was born. The woman said she never talked much about her own parents except to say they died when she was very young and that was why she had been raised by her grandparents."

Bill immediately sensed Sally's heart begin to beat faster. He put his arm around her, gently stroking her. He could tell she was fighting for self-control. Knowing that Angelina was oblivious to anything but what she was hearing from Mr. Armstrong and her own feelings, he carefully squeezed Sally's arm. *"Let's go slowly with this, honey."* Sally swallowed and nodded her head slightly.

Mr. Armstrong pulled out some more papers and continued. "The neighbor thought your father might have been a student at Appleton University or maybe even one of the professors. Your mother never mentioned his name to her. I personally do not think the neighbor's suspicions of who your father may have been are correct. I am more inclined to think that something happened to your father and your mother came to Appleton to go to school, discovered she was pregnant with you, and remained there after you were born, trying to work, raise you, and go to school part time."

He then paused to hand a photocopy of a page out of the University yearbook to Bill and continued. "There's no record of an Elizabeth Beacon as a student, but you can see there was an Elizabeth Eloise Browner. Unfortunately there's no picture."

Bill took the copy and handed it to Sally. She took the paper from him, trying hard to keep her hand from shaking.

Mr. Armstrong closed his file folder and reached for one of the piles of papers sitting on the table. "I checked further with Social Services and they have no record of any other relatives. So, if you don't have any questions, you can sign these papers, and I will file them with the courthouse in Appleton and barring any unforeseen issues, we should be able to get the final signed papers from the court within two weeks." Mr. Armstrong leaned back in his chair and smiled with satisfaction.

Angelina jumped up from her chair and flung herself at Bill and Sally. She was laughing and crying all at the same time. After several moments of joint hugging, Angelina turned to Mr. Armstrong, smiling, and asked, "Where do I sign?"

CHAPTER NINETEEN

A SLIGHT SETBACK

Jordan, Angelina, and Abby sat at a table in the cafeteria close to the door. Angelina had been filling them in on what had happened at the attorney's office the previous day. Angelina and Abby were still eating since they had both done more talking than eating. Jordan laughed as Angelina described the look on the attorney's face when she asked, "Where do I sign."

"Bill said the name Browner that Mr. Armstrong mentioned was familiar to him, so he's checking it out over at the county seat. He says there was a family named Browner that lived up in the hills, but they kept pretty much to themselves. They're gone now, I guess, so it won't really make any difference, but he's just curious to see if it's the same family."

Pushing his chair back, Jordan stood and picked up his tray to return it. Turning he ran into Jason, knocking his tray to the floor, spilling his food all over the floor and Jason.

Jordan looked with horror at Jason. "Hey, Jason, I'm really

sorry! I didn't see you coming!"

Jordan started to bend over to pick up the dropped tray, but Jason gave him a shove. "Yeah right; well this detention is almost over so you better start watching your back." Travis and Austin both snickered but stopped when Jason turned on them, shoving the two of them out of his way. All three boys stared as Jason stormed out of the lunchroom.

Mrs. Aims grabbed both Travis and Austin by the arm and suggested they help clean up the mess on the floor. Jordan was already picking up his tray and empty milk carton that had slid across the floor. Travis and Austin grumbled the whole time, shooting angry looks in Jordan's direction. He returned to the table after dropping off his tray and sat down in utter dejection. "This is perfect, just perfect! So, I guess I'm right back at square one again. This is ridiculous, a total waste of time!"

Angelina looked at Jordan, surprised at the mounting anger in his voice. "Well, aren't we the pot calling the kettle black? In case you didn't notice, Jason also shoved Travis and Austin before he stormed out of here. Did it ever occur to you that maybe something else is going on with Jason, something totally unrelated to you?"

Jordan stared open-mouthed at Angelina. Abby's eyebrows had become upside-down V's and she quickly started eating her salad, staring at her plate. Angelina's eyes flashed, challenging Jordan to say something.

Jordan continued to stare at Angelina, and then his shoulders caved. Shaking his head, he picked up his backpack and stood. "I need to stop at my locker. See ya at class."

Angelina watched Jordan slowly walk out of the lunchroom. Abby swallowed her bite of salad and said, "You were a little hard on him, weren't you?"

~ CHAPTER NINETEEN ~

Angelina turned to Abby, her own emotions and misgivings getting the better of her. "Maybe, but if he's going to cave every time Jason has a little hissy-fit without at least trying to understand what Jason may be going through at the moment, he's not going to be of any help to himself, let alone Jason. I'm not saying it was OK for Jason to get mad, but I think Jason is trying to change, so maybe we need to cut him some slack and see if maybe the better course of action would be a hand instead of a kick."

Abby stood and began gathering up her stuff; she appeared slightly miffed at Angelina's quick jump to Jason's defense and seeming abandonment of Jordan. "I guess you're right. Just don't forget, maybe Jordan's going through something too, and maybe he also needs a hand instead of a kick."

Angelina was fuming inside as she watched Abby walk away. *Well, I'm going through something, too!*

Ten minutes later, Jordan, Angelina, and Abby all arrived at Mr. Allen's European History class. As Jordan slid into the desk next to Angelina, she turned to him and they both spoke at once. "I'm sorry!" Angelina's eyes twinkled as he grinned at her. Abby leaned over her desk so she could see both of them and heaved a big sigh. Angelina looked around at her and laughed.

Austin and Travis came into class and slipped into their seats just before the bell rang. Jordan sighed as Mr. Allen closed the door and walked over to his desk. Jason's seat remained empty the entire class period.

When the bell rang for the end of the period, Austin and Travis were the first out the door, but not before they heard Mr. Allen ask Jordan to remain after class. Jordan could hear them laughing as they walked out. Angelina touched his arm just before she and Abby left for P.E. She smiled as he looked up at her. *"Keep the faith"*.

Jordan nodded and then walked over to Mr. Allen's desk.

Mr. Allen waited until they were alone then asked Jordan to sit down. Mr. Allen sat on the edge of his desk, looked at Jordan, and finally cleared his throat.

"Jordan, Jason came to see me during lunch. He told me what happened in the lunchroom." He waited for a moment, as Jordan seemed to visibly cave, shaking his head with frustration and disappointment. He then continued. "Jordan, I excused Jason from class today because he was very upset about his mom. The biopsy came back positive, so she has to have surgery. Jason doesn't know yet how to process his feelings. When he's afraid or upset, he lashes out. You just happened to be in his direct path today. I think underneath he really knows you didn't dump his lunch on purpose or try to make a fool out of him. Why do you think he pushed Austin and Travis and walked away from them too? Don't give up on this, OK?"

Angelina's words from lunch rang in his ear. *"Well. aren't we the pot calling the kettle black? In case you didn't notice, Jason also shoved Travis and Austin before he stormed out of here. Did it ever occur to you that maybe something else is going on with Jason, something totally unrelated to you?"* Jordan blushed slightly and looked up at Mr. Allen, who was watching him intently.

"OK, Mr. Allen, I'll do my best."

Jordan stood up and started to leave. "Jordan?" Mr. Allen said. "I'm impressed you didn't try to explain or defend yourself. You hang in there, OK?"

Jordan nodded.

The bell rang just as Jordan came into the gym. Greg, who was Mr. Timson's student aide, waved him over to the bleachers. Jordan climbed up and sat down beside him. Jason was sitting between Travis and Austin and did not look at him when he came in. Greg handed him two sheets of paper. Each sheet had a diagram of the two new plays Mr. Timson wanted to incorporate into their last game. The last eight weeks had been dedicated solely to the study of how the game of football was played and won.

Mr. Timson pulled a large dry erase board out on the gym floor. He immediately started drawing the first diagram on the board, explaining how the play was to work.

Greg leaned close to Jordan and whispered, "How come Morton's in a bad mood? Thought things were clearing up between the two of you?"

Jordan whispered back, "They are; he's just going through some tough stuff right now. It'll be OK." Jordan glanced over at Jason, only to see him looking back at him with angry, suspicious eyes.

Greg turned to see Jason glaring at them. "Are you sure about that?"

Jordan sighed as Jason turned back to Travis and slapped him on the back, laughing loudly at the comical question Travis had just asked Mr. Timson about the play. "I hope so."

~

Angelina and Jordan sat side by side in study hall Friday afternoon working on their Physical Science questions that had to be done for class on Monday. Jordan had wanted to have his assignment finished by the end of class since their last game was tonight, and right afterward was the last detention session, which was the overnight campout. He was struggling to keep his mind on his work.

Angelina sat with her book open. She had just finished her last question and was pretending to be rereading the questions and rechecking her answers, when in fact she was really watching Jordan. His thoughts were so loud in her head it was like he was speaking out loud to a room full of people.

Jordan was trying to rationalize to himself that the football practice sessions had not been too bad. *Jason really hasn't singled me out or let Travis and Austin at me either. They have been talking and looking at me a lot. Could they be planning something for detention tonight, while we're on the hike? Maybe I'm just being paranoid. Jason must really be worried about his mom right now. I bet his old man is almost impossible to live with. Maybe I should talk to Mr. Allen again. I could try to see him right after study hall. Maybe I should try to talk to Jason. No, maybe I better not. I don't want them thinking I'm getting weak about this. Gosh, I wish this was over with! I wonder what's going to happen when it is. I wonder if Jason will go back to being the way he was before the fight. How could he? What about what he wrote for Creative Writing? How could he write something that amazing and it all be an act? Could he have been faking it this whole time?*

Angelina reached a trembling hand over and touched Jordan's arm. The look in her eyes told him that she knew everything he had just been mulling over in his head. Angelina bit her bottom lip. "Jordan?"

Jordan jerked his hand free, glaring at her, and whispered through gritted teeth, "I need to work this out myself, OK?"

Jordan angrily stuffed his papers and books into his backpack.

Angelina sat with her hands open, palms up, tears on her cheeks. She closed her eyes and concentrated hard. *"OK, Jordan. If that's the way you want it."*

Jordan turned slowly in his seat and stared at her. *"I could hear you and you weren't even touching me!"*

As the bell rang they both stood up. Neither of them said a

word. They just stood there, looking into each other's eyes. Finally Angelina turned and picked up her papers and book, put them in her backpack, and walked away from Jordan. *"Good luck tonight at the game; I'll be cheering for you."*

Abby caught up with Angelina at the door and looked back at Jordan before she followed her out into the hall. He was still standing at the table staring after Angelina.

"Everything OK with you two?" Abby asked as she hurried along side of Angelina.

"No, but it's out of my hands now." Angelina stopped walking abruptly, causing Abby to almost run into her. She turned to look at her, worry and frustration bringing an edge to her voice. "I'm really worried about this last detention session. I think Jason is about to snap!"

Abby looked at her thoughtfully for a moment, then asked, "Have you talked to Bill and Sally about this yet?"

Angelina's eyes lit up as she started walking fast again toward her locker. "That's what I'm going to do right now!"

Angelina was running up the back steps just as Bill pulled his truck into the driveway. She spun around to look at him. Bill got out of the truck and held his hands out in front of him, as if for protection, laughing.

Angelina was fighting back tears. "It's not funny, Dad!" Sally stood holding the door open for them. *"Come inside, Angelina. Bill, stop laughing."*

Bill and Angelina sat down at the counter in the kitchen while Sally continued dipping apples in caramel, rolling them in nuts and then placing them on wax paper on the counter. The smell of fresh apples and warm caramel made Angelina's stomach growl. Struggling to keep from crying, Angelina quickly told Bill and Sally everything that happened, starting with lunch. How Jason had not come to Mr. Allen's class, and what Mr. Allen told Jordan about Jason's mom after class. How Jason had acted in P.E., and last of all, what had happened between herself and Jordan in study hall.

Bill listened patiently while Angelina recounted everything in great detail. When she finally paused for breath, he spoke. "I have to agree with Mr. Allen's opinion. Finding out that his mother for sure had cancer and will now have to have major surgery with probably some kind of radiation treatments afterward must have really thrown Jason a curve. He was very upset, just lashing out."

Sally set the last caramel apple on the wax paper and went to the sink to rinse off her hands. Drying her hands on a towel, she turned to Angelina. "I think that Jordan is right too. He has to work this out himself. I know you want to jump in there and try to 'fix' things for him, but he really needs to do it himself, honey." Angelina opened her mouth to protest, but Sally held up her hand. "No, really, Angelina, if you don't let him, he's going to end up resenting you for it. You just need to be there for him when he comes to you."

Angelina reached for a caramel apple. "It's just that I'm scared for Jordan."

Bill and Sally both said in unison, "You have to believe in him, Angelina. Believe he is going to be able to handle the situation."
Angelina sat staring at the apple on the stick. The caramel was still soft to the touch. "I guess I don't really have any doubts that Jordan can handle any situation that might come up, it's Jason I'm worried about." She took a bite out of the apple, dripping soft caramel down her chin.

Sally started laughing and handed her a napkin. Bill coughed into his hand, trying not to laugh, and commented, "Well, Jason is going through a tough time, but I think he really is changing, and more important, he wants to change."

Sally was now holding onto the counter for support, laughing hysterically at Angelina. The juice from the apple, mixed with the still soft caramel was making a mess of her face. Bill covered his face with his hands and tried to muffle the snorting sound he was making. Angelina tried to catch a drip of caramel with her tongue, then grabbed up the napkin to wipe her face, rolling her eyes at both of them as she mumbled, "Maybe I should have waited a little longer before trying to eat one of these."

Bill put his arm around her shoulder, gave her a squeeze, and then kissed her on the forehead, avoiding her still sticky face. "You're a real stitch, Angelina girl!"

Sally handed Angelina a damp cloth and said, "We thought we'd go to the game again tonight, if it's OK with you."

Angelina, who was mopping her face, stopped and looked at Sally in wonder. "Of course it's OK, Mom. Why, you and Dad can even sit with me!" Angelina laughed as Sally threw a towel at her, then headed upstairs to change for the game.

Bill, who was standing at the back door watching Sally, smiled to himself. *"Look at you. You're grinning so big I'm scared your face is going to crack."*

Sally, hearing his thoughts, picked up the towel and threw it at him just before he ducked out the door laughing.

CHAPTER TWENTY

FROM VICTORIOUS GAME TO LAST DETENTION

Angelina tried to concentrate on the game but found she was watching Jason, trying to read his thoughts, to see if he had any hidden agenda. Because of the excitement of the game, the only thing she was getting were jumbled thoughts about the plays and the thrill of the game. She sighed, feeling helpless to do anything.

Sally slipped her arm around her and yelled above the screaming crowd, "The team's really playing well together, don't you think?"

Bill suddenly jumped to his feet yelling, almost knocking over the cup of hot cider Angelina was holding. Angelina caught Jordan's thought. *"Way to go, Jason!"*

Jason had grabbed the ball when one of the Kingston Knights had fumbled. The crowd was now screaming with excitement as Jason ran the full 40 yards for the last touchdown of the game. As he crossed the line he slammed the ball to the ground and ran in place with both arms strait up in the air. The scoreboard showed Home - 35, Kingston Knights - 18, with only forty-five seconds remaining on the clock.

As the guys re-huddled for their last play, Greg looked around at his team members. "OK, we have forty-five seconds on the clock, and a seventeen point lead. I know we don't need the points, but I would still rather do the two-point conversion play over the extra point play. So, Jordan, let's have you run the ball this time; Jason, I want you to do the fake-off maneuver."

Jordan cleared his throat, pointedly not looking at Jason. "Greg, I think we should keep Jason running the ball. The Knights know we did this play last week and they'll be expecting us to 'switch' runners."

Greg looked thoughtfully at Jordan without speaking. He gave a quick nod of his head. "OK, we run the play like Jordan says." They broke their huddle with a shout and lined up for the play.

With the restarting of the clock, Greg called out the numbers and did a quick under-toss of the ball to Jason, then turned and did a fake pass toward Jordan, who was already running. Jason had the ball over the line for the two-point conversion score before the Knights knew what happened.

The Baker's Bluff crowd erupted in screams and cheers, horns blowing and popcorn flying in the air. The cheerleaders started a chant for the countdown of the last six seconds on the clock and the crowd joined in. The blasting of the buzzer signaled the end of the game. As the guys pounded and jumped on each other, Jason and Jordan found themselves facing each other amid the screaming confusion surrounding them. They both stood looking at each other. Suddenly Jordan grinned and held out his hand toward Jason. Jason's looked relieved as he grabbed Jordan's arm in a firm clasp.

~ FROM VICTORIOUS GAME TO LAST DETENTION ~

Austin and Travis came from out of nowhere and began pounding on Jason, laughing and shouting, and then the three of them were walking off the field together. As Jordan watched them go Jason turned to look back at him, and grinning, gave him a 'thumbs-up' signal. Jordan grinned and signaled back and then turned to look up at the bleachers. It took only a moment to spot Bill, Sally and Angelina. Sally was waving madly. Bill was giving him a thumbs-up and he could hear him clearly in his head. *"Great game, Jordan! Remember, if you ever need help, just call out to me, I'll hear you. We'll see you tomorrow after detention. Everything's going to work out!"*

Jordan nodded and then looked at Angelina. *"Thanks for cheering for me, Angelina."* He turned quickly and ran to catch up with Greg and walked to the locker room with him.

As they changed in the locker room, Greg looked over at Jordan. "Ya know, we probably still could have won that last play with you taking the ball, but I have to admit, it was a good plan. They were expecting you to have the ball. You're going to make a great team captain for the next two years."

Jordan looked surprised. "Ya mean it?"

"Yes, I do. You have what it takes. You're impartial and you think only about what is best for the whole team. That's what the team captain has to do. Think of the team and not about himself." He grinned. "OK, you can think about yourself a little bit." He laughed as Jordan threw a towel at him.

It took Jordan ten minutes to change, gather up his camping gear, and walk out to the front of the school where Mr. Allen had said he would be waiting for the boys with his Land Rover. As Jordan approached Mr. Allen, he thought about Greg's parting words. *"Good luck, tonight. Just keep thinking about the group as a whole and everything will work out all right."*

Mr. Allen opened the back of his SUV so Jordan could put his stuff in; then they waited for Jason, Austin, and Travis. The boys came out the front of the school moments later, toting their gear. Once it was loaded, they all climbed in and headed out to Mr. Allen's place.

Mr. Allen kept all four boys busy answering questions about the game. As he drove up to the house, the boys could see four brand-new hiking packs sitting on the front porch. Mr. Allen shut off the engine and turned around in his seat to look at the surprised and excited faces of the boys. "OK, look, you can't let this get around or I'm going to be having everyone in the school wanting to get put into detention with me. Besides, you fellows have worked pretty hard these last three weeks. I've gotten a lot of work out of you. So, let's just keep a lid on this, OK? Well, what are you waiting for? Go on, you can each pick out the pack you want and store your gear while I go inside and get mine."

Jason, Jordan, Austin, and Travis climbed out of the Land Rover and rushed up on the porch to check out the packs. There were other piles on the porch; tents, blankets, pans, axes, ropes, and food, which would all be divided between them. Once all their stuff was packed, Mr. Allen made sure they each had a map, a compass, and bottles of water, flashlights, and fire-making material.

"It will take us roughly thirty minutes to hike to our first stopping point. We'll rest for about five minutes and then it will be another thirty minutes to the next stopping point. Everyone got their packs strapped on correctly? OK, let's go."

Once through the gate by the barn, the boys walked single file behind Mr. Allen across the field; Travis was right behind Mr.

~FROM VICTORIOUS GAME TO LAST DETENTION~

Allen, then Austin, followed by Jason, with Jordan bringing up the rear. The almost clear night sky was a spectacular display of twinkling stars. The full moon brought a brightness that disguised the lateness of the hour. The distant hooting of an owl was the only other noise besides the crunching of their feet on the leaves on the ground and the voices of Travis and Austin talking to Mr. Allen. Jordan followed silently, listening to Travis and Austin's back and forth banter of everything from how the game went to arguing about the kinds of wild animals they might see before the end of their trip. Jason was silent, not joining in with their laughing and storytelling.

Since there really wasn't a trail, Jordan picked up his pace just enough so he was able to walk beside Jason. They continued on in silence for about twenty steps, when Jordan ventured, "That was a good game tonight, Jason."

Jason was silent for a moment. "Yeah, it was a good game. Probably could have been better though. A couple of those balls you passed to me you could have gone ahead and run your self. Why didn't you?"

Jordan looked over at him, grinning. "I guess I could have run them, but you *are* a *little* faster than me and I did have someone very close on my tail. Guess I just felt we were finally working as a real team tonight. I knew you could finish off the play and score for us and that was the most important thing."

Jason was silent for a moment then suddenly stopped walking and turned to Jordan. "Listen, Jordan, I'm sorry about what I said today in the lunchroom and how I acted later in the gym." He paused to clear his throat. "It's just that, well, things are a little tough at home right now..." His voice broke and he looked away.

Jordan stood silently beside him, kicking at stones on the

ground. "Jason, I know things don't look good right now. But you've got to have faith that they've caught this thing early enough, and with treatment besides the surgery, I'm sure your mom's going to be just fine."

Jason looked back at Jordan, his face a mixture of emotions. Jordan met his gaze and didn't look away, even as tears began to spill down Jason's cheeks. They could both hear Travis and Austin laughing in the distant shadows ahead of them. Jordan reached out and took hold of Jason's arm, keeping his voice low and serious. "You wait here a second and let me go on ahead of you. You can catch up with us in a couple of minutes. OK?"

Jason nodded without speaking.

Jordan hurried ahead several yards then slowed down so Jason wouldn't have a long way to come to catch up. His heart was pounding hard. He was sure Travis and Austin had not noticed anything.

"Good job, Jordan!"

Jordan's head jerked around. *"Bill, is that you?"* Jordan shivered in the resounding silence that followed.

CHAPTER TWENTY-ONE

A WONDERFUL DISCISCOVERY

Angelina sat cross-legged in her warm flannel pajamas on the couch in the family room; Alex curled up on her lap purring contentedly. Beside her, on the couch, lay the photo album that Sally had started shortly after Angelina came to live with them. There were pictures of her with Alex in the tire swing, and some of her building the tree house with Bill and Jordan. Angelina smiled at the picture of her and Sally, both of them covered with flour. They had been making cookies and somehow ended up having a flour fight. What a sight the kitchen had been. Bill had laughed at them till he slipped on the flour on the floor and landed on his backside, creating a puffy cloud of flour in the air. Sally had caught that priceless picture on film.

Angelina turned the page to see a picture of herself in PJ's, standing in front of a huge Christmas tree, holding a very large stocking stuffed full of candy, fruit, and special little gifts. To this day there were still gifts from "Santa" under the tree, even though

~ CHAPTER TWENTY-ONE ~

Jordan had told her the day after her tenth birthday that there was no "real" Santa. They had gotten into a big argument over it and Jordan had grabbed her brand-new Barbie doll by the head. They had both pulled, struggling to keep hold of the doll, thus the head had come off. Angelina remembered standing, holding the headless doll, staring at it in horror. She had started crying and threw the doll at Jordan and ran into the house. Jordan tried for almost a half hour to get the head back on. Bill found him later up in the tree house, crying. Bill fiddled with the doll and worked "a little magic" and got the head back on.

Angelina smiled, remembering how Jordan had brought the doll back to her. She knew that Bill had found him in the tree house crying and that Bill had fixed the doll. She had still been mad at Jordan and had wanted to call him a crybaby. But when she had looked up at him, standing in the doorway, holding out the doll to her, he had looked so lost and dejected that she had just reached out and took the doll. He had stood there, his hands jammed into his jeans pockets, scuffing the toe of his shoe on the rug. He'd finally spoken, "I'm really sorry, Angelina, I didn't mean to break your doll's head off. Bill fixed it for you. I'm sorry I made you cry."

He had not made her cry again, until the other night when they were popping corn in the fireplace.

Angelina turned the page and laughed out loud at the picture of Papaw Jake, Bill's dad, throwing her off the dock into the lake up at High Ridge. Papaw Jake and Mamaw Emma - - Bill's parents - - until two years ago had lived in a high valley they called High Ridge. Their big log home was on a beautiful lake that Bill said did not have a bottom, that's how deep it was. The water was always cold, but that was OK on hot summer days. Angelina spent most of her summers at High Ridge; it was where Bill had taught her to swim and ride horses.

Jordan spent most of his summers there too.

Now Jake and Emma lived in Florida. They still came every summer, just before Memorial Day, and stayed up at the lake all summer. They went back to Florida right after Labor Day but came back the week of Thanksgiving, and stayed with Bill and Sally till just after Christmas. They would be here for Angelina's birthday. She could hardly wait.

Angelina smiled as she looked at the next picture of her and Jordan on the dock. She was holding an eighteen-inch trout and Jordan was holding a string of smaller fish. She looked up as Bill and Sally came into the family room. Sally picked up the album and sat down on the couch beside her. Bill sat down on a cushion that he had tossed down on the floor.

"What ya looking at?" Bill asked. He snapped his fingers and Alex stood up and jumped down from the couch and came over to him to curl up in his lap.

"I've just been looking back over the pictures you've taken since I came to live here. I don't remember a whole lot before that. I have some memories of my mother, of living in an apartment with her. You both know, I've already told you before, what I could remember. I guess I was hoping to maybe jog my memory for more memories by looking at these old photos."

Sally laughed out loud. "Look at this one, Angelina; you and Papaw Jake are both trying to eat that great big turkey leg at the same time!" Angelina laughed, remembering the struggle that had ensued over that huge juicy drumstick. Mamaw Emma had finally wrestled the leg from them and then took a bite herself, bringing roars of protest from them both.

After a moment she asked, "Do they know you are trying to adopt me?"

Bill laughed. "Are you kidding? They've been hinting to us to do it for almost three years now."

Angelina looked at Bill. "So...why *did* you wait so long?" Bill looked at Sally. Angelina turned to look at Sally. "What are you blocking from me now?"

Sally sighed and took hold of her hands. "Angelina, we are not deliberately keeping anything from you. We just wanted to be absolutely sure of something before we told you." Sally looked at Bill for help.

Bill leaned forward. "Angelina, what we are checking out will not keep us from adopting you. If anything, it will cinch it. But either way, ***WE WANT YOU!*** And *THAT* is what we want you to know and believe, with all your heart!"

They sat for several more minutes on the couch, slowly turning the pages, laughing at pictures, and remembering all the good memories from the past six years.

Angelina turned the last page to look at the picture Sally had just put in the book. It was of her and Jordan standing in the entryway, dressed as Peter Pan and Tinker Bell. She smiled, remembering how excited Evelyn had been when she had gently 'fluttered' through the air down to the floor. Nothing seemed to faze her. She was not scared of them, nor did she think the fact they had special abilities was something bad or terrible. Why couldn't everyone be like Evelyn?

Angelina looked up at Sally, who was staring into the fire. She seemed to be trying to make up her mind about something. Suddenly Sally stood up and walked over to the cabinet in the corner of the family room. She opened a drawer and dug around till she pulled out a small photo album that Angelina had never seen before. She came back over and sat down beside her again.

"I've had a suspicion about something for about a year now, ever since you started to change in your appearance. You know, when you began losing your 'little girl' look and started looking more and more like a young woman."

Angelina blushed but continued to look at Sally, waiting for her to continue. Sally sat for a moment, the book still closed on her lap, looking off into the distance, like she was looking back across time.

"I had a little sister. Our parents died in a farming accident when we were very young. I barely remember them. After their death, our grandparents, who lived high up in the mountains raised us." Angelina caught her breath in a sudden gasp as Sally continued. "They were very fearful folks, Angelina. They could remember the terrible things done to some of the people of Baker's Bluff who were 'different.' We pretty much kept to ourselves. Grandma taught us at home till the county came and said we had to go to public school. My little sister was just fifteen, your age, Angelina, when she ran away. At first I could still talk to her. I didn't know where she was, but I knew she was OK. Then she met someone. She started blocking me, and then she was gone from my mind."

She opened the album, gazing at it as she continued with her story. "This is the only picture I have of my grandparents, my sister, and myself. It was a picture that I always kept with me on my person. So, when the fire burned our home in the mountains, killing Grandma and Grandpa, when I was eighteen, leaving me all alone, well, this was all I had of my family history." She laughed softly. "I remember the day this picture was taken. We propped the camera on a log and used the timer so that I could run and get in the picture too. The camera had been my sixteenth birthday present. Elizabeth was fourteen when I took this picture." Angelina caught her breath again, staring in wonder at Sally. "She ran away the next summer, when she turned fifteen. Gramps was a hard man, but you have to understand Angelina, he'd seen so much. See?" Sally handed the album to Angelina. "You could be her twin sister, Angelina."

Angelina stared silently at what looked to be a very old black-and-white photograph of herself beside an old man and woman, and a much younger Sally. She looked up at Sally, her face pale with shock.

"I believe with all my heart, Angelina, that you are my sister's child."

Bill leaned over and touched Angelina's arm. She looked at him, her eyes still large with wonder. "Angelina, we have wanted to make you our own for a long time. Then, when you started changing, well, we began to think that maybe, just maybe you really did belong to us. But we want you to know, that even if it turns out that you are not Elizabeth's daughter, although I think that highly unlikely given the strong resemblance between the two of you, we want you anyway, because we love you, and as far as we're concerned, ***you are our daughter!*** "

Angelina looked closely at the picture in the photo album. Slowly she laid it in her lap, closed her eyes, and slowed her breathing way down....

She was back in the shopping cart in the store. Slowly she raised her head and tried to focus on her mother's face. She looked tired and strained, but it was definitely the same face, just slightly older, than the face in the picture. Her mother's hand reached out and gently stroked her head. When she smiled, her whole face seemed to light up.

Angelina said softly, "Momma?"

Angelina drew in a deep breath and opened her eyes. Bill and

Sally were each holding onto one of her arms. Both were looking at her. Sally had tears streaming down her cheeks. "Thank you, Angelina. I saw her. Your mother *was* my sister! I finally now know what happened to her. I know I can never take her place, but I hope you will still call me mom."

Tears were now streaming down Angelina's face. "You ***ARE*** my mom and dad now! I'm sure this is what my momma would have wanted."

CHAPTER TWENTY-TWO

THE WRONG TRAIL

Almost ten minutes passed before Jason finally caught up with Jordan again. They walked silently side by side for about twenty steps before Jason finally spoke. "Thanks, Jordan. Ya know, I think I've really had you pegged wrong."

Jordan grinned, "Yeah? Well, you've been a little confusing to me too. I have to say though, you're turning out to be OK." Jordan laughed and playfully punched Jason in the arm.

Jason grinned. "Ya know, hanging with you is probably gonna ruin my reputation."

Jordan laughed again, nodding. "Yeah, it probably will."

Travis suddenly yelled from several yards ahead that Mr. Allen wanted them to catch up. Jason looked at Jordan as they picked up their pace. "So, do you think there's any hope for those too goofballs?"

Jordan slapped him on the back. "Jason, if I've learned one thing these last four weeks it's that there is always HOPE!"

After a couple of minutes they caught up with Mr. Allen, Travis, and Austin. They had all been walking for well over a half an hour. It was completely dark out, but the almost full moon and nearly cloudless sky made for a fairly easy hike to their first stopping point.

Mr. Allen said they would rest for five minutes, look over the map, and then set out for the next stopping point. He said it would take at least another thirty minutes of hiking to reach it. "Did you all remember to bring your assignment with you? How the different fuels can affect the different relationships in our life?"

They all echoed, "Yes!"

"Well, I want you to think about that during this next leg of our hike."

During their last detention at Mr. Allen's house they had spent time learning how to use the special maps Mr. Allen had provided. They learned how to locate places on the map from directional coordinates that Mr. Allen gave them.

There were large boulders where they had stopped to rest. Mr. Allen gave them the end directional coordinates for where they were going to end up and asked them to pair up. Travis and Austin looked at each other, and grinning, moved off to one of the boulders to spread out their maps. Jordan looked at Jason. "I guess we're pairing up." Jason grinned, "Yeah, the winning combo!"

As the boys studied the map, they could see that there were three different routes to the campsite from their next stopping point. All three routes looked OK, but the most challenging one seemed to be the one that forked to the left. Jordan and Jason looked at each other and grinned. They walked over to Mr. Allen to tell him that was the trail they wanted to take.

Travis and Austin decided on the middle trail, so Mr. Allen said he would take the trail to the right, and they were off again for the second third of the hike.

The farther they walked the more challenging the trail became. The different night sounds indicated they were getting deeper into the wild. Jason and Jordan still walked side by side.

Jordan stepped over a large rock and looked at Jason. "Your essay paper for Creative Writing was really great, Jason. It sure made me stop and think. What you said is so true." Jordan stooped to pick up a stick and tossed it into the darkness off the trail. "It really doesn't matter what the circumstances are that lead up to a choice that we make. We make the choice and nobody else. That's tough to swallow, but it's the truth." Jordan picked up another stick and gave it a heave. He looked sheepishly over at Jason. "Ya know, I've made some stupid choices that I can't blame on anyone but myself. Yeah, you really hit the nail on the head with your paper."

Jason walked along in silence, kicking stones out of his way. "Well, your paper was quite something too. I think that's one of my big problems. I've 'what-ifed' myself into more messes than I care to remember or admit to. It's just so easy to do, ya know? You made me stop and think though. That in itself is really something!" Jason laughed as Jordan turned and gave him a thumbs-up.

It did not seem like it had been thirty minutes when Mr. Allen had them stop to rest again. Jordan looked at his watch in the beam of his flashlight, 10:45; it just did not feel that late. Mr. Allen said it would probably take them another thirty minutes to reach the final campsite that he had decided on. "I advise you to stick together. It is very important that you work together as a team if you want to reach the final campsite. I want to stress that this is NOT a race to see who can get to the campsite first." Mr. Allen looked around at their grinning faces and nodding heads and shook his head, sighing before he continued. "Once we are at the site we will need to collect firewood and set up the tents and start a *SAFE* fire. We practiced that a lot, so let's try not to burn down the mountain. OK? Does everyone have his compass? Are all your flashlights working?" As the boys hollered out yes, Mr. Allen looked at his watch. "Well, it's now 10:50. So, I'll see you all at the campsite in about a half an hour." He then picked up his walking stick, turned, and headed off up the right fork trail.

Austin and Travis looked nervously at each other, and then took off down the center trail. Jason and Jordan watched them disappear into the darkness, and then they headed off down the left fork. They had walked almost one hundred feet when the trail narrowed, and it became obvious that one of them would have to lead and the other follow. Jordan stopped walking and turned to Jason. "Why don't you take the lead?" Grinning he added, "I'll watch your back." Jason looked at him for a moment, and then headed off up the trail at a fast pace.

They had been walking for a good ten minutes when the terrain started to become a little more difficult to maneuver. Jordan kept stopping to check his compass to verify the direction they were going as the trail was now twisting and turning back and forth on itself multiple times. Shortly they came to another fork in the trail. Neither could remember Mr. Allen mentioning another fork. Both boys stopped and consulted the map. They could not find the second fork on the map.

"Great!" The hint of panic in Jason's voice warned Jordan to take it slow.

Jordan looked at his compass thoughtfully. "Ya know, from the final coordinates that Mr. Allen gave us I think we want to be going in a north-westerly direction. According to the compass I'm guessing we are probably gonna want to take the left fork."

~ CHAPTER TWENTY-TWO ~

Jason spun around to look at Jordan. "How do you know, smart guy that ten feet down the trail it's not going to twist and turn on us again?"

Jordan paused before replying, trying to fight back his own rising panic, feeling frustration and resentment that Jason could so quickly turn on him. "I don't. I guess after a hundred yards or so I figured we'd probably know if we needed to turn around and come back to the other trail. So, do you want to flip a coin to see which one we try first?" *Just keep on believing the best, believe the best.*

Jason turned to look at the two trails again. "Are you serious? I already know which trail is the correct one to take. You're right that we need to end up north west of here so it's obviously the right-hand fork that we need to take."

Jordan again took a moment to shake off his desire for a quick reply. "Ok. Right fork it is. You want to keep leading?"

Jason looked at the map again and then at his compass. It was obvious to Jordan that Jason was now questioning his choice of which fork to take. He waited silently.

In the end Jason's pride won out. Pointing his flashlight out in front of him, he set off down the right-hand fork at a fast pace.

Shaking his head, Jordan sighed and slowly followed.

CHAPTER TWENTY-THREE

THE ACCIDENT

Angelina woke with a start to the sounds of Bill and Sally getting out of bed.

"OK, Jordan, you have ropes with you, right?"

"Yes."

"Where is Mr. Allen?"

"He had us choose different trails to take. We paired up and we're supposed to meet at the campsite."

"What happened?"

"We took a wrong fork. Mr. Allen didn't mention that we would have a fork in the trail we took, and we took the wrong one."

"Can you see Jason?"

"Yes. He must be unconscious because he doesn't answer when I call out to him."

"Can you reach him?"

"I think so, but I won't be able to get him back up here by myself."

~ CHAPTER TWENTY-THREE ~

"OK. I don't know how long it will take us to get there, but we're coming. Try to reach him and keep him warm. Don't move him too much. You can't be too sure how badly he's hurt. I'll be in touch."

Angelina was already pulling on jeans and boots when Sally knocked on the door and came into her room. "You heard?"

"Yes. Is Jordan OK? What happened?" Angelina pulled a sweatshirt on over her long sleeve shirt.

"You know as much as we do, honey. We'll meet you downstairs in five minutes." Sally closed the door as she hurried back to her and Bill's room.

Twenty minutes later they pulled up the drive of the Allen farm. Chief James Waits pulled in right behind them.

Mrs. Allen was in the kitchen. Set out on the table was a large first aid kit, several thermoses of hot coffee, and a map with the three trails marked in different colors, showing which trail each of the boys and Mr. Allen had taken.

Angelina looked at Sally. *"How does she know all this?"* Then she noticed the walkie-talkie on the table.

As they all gathered around the map, Mrs. Allen pointed to the three forks in the trail and said, "Jordan and Jason took the left fork. If you take the horses, you'll get there faster. You're going to have a hard time after that though. They took the wrong fork half a mile up the trail and walked it for almost a mile before Jason finally admitted they had taken the wrong fork. He refused to retrace their path and took off through the woods in the direction he thought the correct trail would be. After another 45 minutes he went a little crazy and ended up going over the edge of a ravine. There are a lot of ravines in the area so it may take a while to find them. The horses are all saddled up down at the barn. Take these things with you, and be careful!"

She walked them to the barn, talking to Bill and Chief Waits. Angelina followed with Sally still trying to sort out *how* Mrs. Allen could know all the stuff she had just told them.

~

Jordan struggled to tie his rope securely around the tree, calling out to Jason. "Jason, Jason, can you hear me? Jason, are you OK?" Jordan's stomach was still in a knot, and he felt sick as he remembered how Jason had turned to look back at him as he stormed forward through the woods. How Jason had let out a terrified yell and suddenly disappeared. Jordan had moved forward cautiously and had still almost missed seeing the edge of the ravine himself. Seeing Jason at the bottom of the ravine, unmoving, had sent chills of terror up and down his spine like no horror movie had ever been able to do.

He directed his flashlight again down into the ravine where Jason had landed. He still hadn't moved. Jordan double-checked his ropes and hooks to be sure they were all secured the way Mr. Allen had taught them for rock climbing. He stood for a moment looking down into the ravine. He glanced over at all his gear lying on the ground near the edge of the ravine. *I can get down there, but what about all that stuff? I may need some of it till help gets here.* Jordan walked over and picked up his third length of rope. Carefully he tied it to his waist, securing the other end to his tent and bedroll. Then he picked up his backpack and put it on, carefully hooking the straps and hooks so they would not interfere with his climbing gear. Back at the edge of the ravine, he again pointed the flashlight down on Jason, who still had not moved. It was a good ten feet to the bottom of the ravine, and Jason had rolled a little farther. Jordan took a deep breath, *OK; I can do this, I can do this.* He then slowly eased over the edge of the ravine.

~ CHAPTER TWENTY-THREE ~

Five minutes later Jordan's feet touched the bottom of the ravine. He quickly unhooked from the rope, shed his gear, checked the perimeter of the area to be sure it was safe, and then checked Jason. He could tell at once that Jason's left leg was broken and he could see a lump on the side of his head. The leg was not bleeding profusely, so he knew no artery had been cut. He took a large handkerchief out of his pack and knotted it around the wound to stop the blood flow. Carefully he pulled up Jason's eyelids and checked the reaction of the pupils to his flashlight. They shrank to pin drops in the light and slowly got bigger as Jordan moved the beam off to the left. He then checked Jason's ears for blood. *None, well, that's a good sign.*

Very carefully, trying not to move him, Jordan felt with his fingers around the back of Jason's neck and head. Nothing felt abnormal. He leaned back on his heels; trying to think of anything he could have forgotten. Suddenly Jason moaned and opened his eyes. With a wild flaying motion he struck out at Jordan but stopped as he cried out in pain.

"Take it easy, Jason. It's me, Jordan. You've had a bad fall, a good ten feet at least. You've got a broken leg, maybe a concussion, and I don't know what else. Don't move. Does your back hurt; do you have feeling in your legs?"

Jason lay panting, his eyes pinched shut. Jordan leaned close and touched Jason's good leg. "Can you feel that?"

"Yes!" Jason answered through gritted teeth.

"Does your back or neck feel strange?" Jordan questioned, concern in his voice.

"No. But I can't tell since I seem to be hurting all over. My head really hurts, and I feel like I might spew any moment." His voice was hedging on hysteria.

Jordan grinned. "Try not to, OK? I think we're in enough of a mess without adding a bad smell to the scene."

Jason opened his eyes and looked at Jordan, his next words dripping with sarcasm. "Well, things can't be too bad if you can talk like that. Guess Mr. Hot Shot's got everything under control. Gonna clean up Mr. Screw-up's mess, huh?"

Jordan, kneeling beside Jason, stopped smiling and stared at him for a moment without speaking. Slowly he started to get up. Jason reached out and grabbed his arm. "Wait a minute. I'm sorry, Jordan. You haven't done anything to deserve what I just said to you. I don't know where that came from. I owe you an apology for getting us into this mess. Between my pride and my 'big foot', my mouth keeps getting me into trouble." He paused for a moment, letting go of Jordan's arm, and then forced a smile, "Maybe you should lead the rest of this hike. I'll follow you, OK?" Jason held out his hand to Jordan, waiting.

Jordan leaned forward so he could look Jason in the eye; he reached out and clasped his hand. "OK, man, it's a deal. Just don't puke on me, OK?"

Jordan stood up and cast his flashlight slowly around the area where Jason lay. It was much darker down in the ravine compared to higher up where they had the full effect of the moon. They really needed to find some cover. Jordan looked back at Jason. "Do you think you could move if I put a splint on your leg?"

Jason looked surprised. "Do you know how to do that?"

"Yeah, I got certified in first aid last summer. I'm hoping to get a job at Baker's Bluff campgrounds this coming summer because I want to buy a car in the fall. I need money for that, and there's no way I'm letting Mom help me at all." He walked back over to where he had dropped his gear.

~ CHAPTER TWENTY-THREE ~

Jason still looked a little worried. "Will it hurt much?" Sighing, Jordan looked back at Jason. "Yeah, it probably will." Jason groaned and then laid back and closed his eyes.

Jordan grabbed his ax to walk around the area again. "Just relax for a minute; I need to find some branches that will work as a splint."

Five minutes later Jordan was back with four branches of wood, all the same length, stripped of their bark. He opened his pack, pulled out a spare T-shirt, and with his knife started cutting and tearing it into strips. Once everything was ready he propped Jason up against both of the backpacks and then gave him a flashlight to hold so he could see. Jordan sat down on the ground facing Jason. He put his left foot up against Jason's right foot. "OK, Jason, I want you to push on my foot with your right leg. I'm going to pull hard on your left leg so the bone will slip back into place. It's going to hurt, so try not to throw the flashlight at me, OK? Now push!"

Jason pushed, looking nervously at Jordan, and started to laugh but yelled in pain as Jordan pulled on his left leg. Jordan could see the bone slip back into place. Quickly he moved to Jason's left side and loosened the handkerchief he had put around the wound. With his knife he cut the torn pant leg open so he could better see the wound, and then carefully cleaned it with water from one of his water bottles. He then rewrapped the wound, lined up the pieces of wood from above Jason's ankle to just above his knee, and began gently wrapping his leg with the remaining strips of the T-shirt.

When he was done he reached over and took the flashlight from a shaking, pale Jason. He smiled encouragingly at him and said, "You did great, Jason. Now just rest a minute while I see if I can find us some decent shelter." Jason nodded, leaned his head back, and closed his eyes.

Jordan walked about fifty feet north of their position and, finding nothing that would work as a shelter, turned around and came back. Jason still sat with his eyes closed, leaning against the backpacks. The night air was getting colder, bringing a sense of urgency to Jordan as he headed south of their position. He walked about twenty-five feet when he spotted what looked like the entrance to a small cave. He remembered Mr. Allen saying there were lots of caves in the area and had been hoping to find one they could use.

The wind started to pick up as he searched the ground and brush outside the cave for any signs of animal activity. Everything looked pretty clean. The tall trees creaked and groaned as an owl hooted somewhere in the darkness, causing him to jump nervously. Cautiously he pointed the flashlight into the cave. Picking up a rock, he tossed it into the cave and listened carefully for any sounds of movement.

After a few minutes he stepped into the cave and shined his flashlight around. The cave was shallow, about forty feet deep. Many of the rocks at the entrance to the cave were moss covered and slippery. The roof sloped toward the ground at the back of the cave. There did not appear to be any passageways leading off the main cavern area. A short distance from the entrance the ground became hard-packed earth, strewn with leaves, twigs, and a few small animal bones. It was dry and sheltered from the wind. Jordan saw a shallow spring a few feet from the entrance to the cave and a natural opening high up in the ceiling over the entrance. *This is perfect,* he thought.

Jordan hurried back to Jason. It didn't look like he had moved at all. As he got close, a small twig snapped under his foot. Jason's eyes opened and he raised his arm up in the air holding a large piece of dead wood.

~ CHAPTER TWENTY-THREE ~

"It's just me, Jason. It's OK. I found us some shelter. Do you think you can stand up if I help you?"

Jason dropped the wood, his eyes reflecting the pain he was in, but he still managed a smile. "With *your* help, I can do anything!" He reached out and grasped Jordan's outstretched hand with both of his, and Jordan carefully lifted him to his feet. Jordan quickly turned and put his arm around Jason's waist to give him more support.

Jason stood still for a moment, trembling slightly. "Let me get my balance a minute and see if the world stops spinning."

Jordan laughed with relief. "Sure, Jason, take your time."

It took them a good five minutes to walk the twenty-five feet to the cave. Jordan had Jason lean up against a tree close to the cave so he could check the cave again to be sure nothing had decided to take up residence since he had left. Once he had Jason in the cave he ran back for all their gear.

Back in the cave again, Jordan gathered up armloads of leaves and made a slight mound with them. Then he laid out Jason's bedroll and settled Jason as comfortably as he could. Jason laid back and shut his eyes, his breathing coming in short gasps as he tried to deal with the pain.

Jordan walked over to his backpack. "Jason, I'm gonna go and get some wood so we can have a fire. Will you be OK? Do you want a drink of water first?"

Jason opened his eyes. "Ya, that would be great; thank you."

Jordan brought him a bottle of water. "Just take a couple of sips, OK? How's the stomach? Still feeling like you could hurl?"

Jason took a small sip, recapped the bottle, and set it beside him on the ground. "A little, but I think I'll be OK. Go get the wood." He leaned his head back and closed his eyes. Suddenly he jerked his head up and looked at Jordan. "Sorry. I forgot I was going to follow you."

Jordan laughed as he headed out to gather wood. "Now I know for sure you're gonna live."

Jordan picked up enough wood to get a fire started. He remembered Mr. Allen's warning to not burn the mountain down and carefully prepared an area near the entrance of the cave. After about twenty minutes he had a decent fire going, the smoke going up through the natural opening at the top of the cave just over the entrance. Jordan stood looking at the small pile of wood, listening to the night sounds outside of the cave. He glanced at Jason.

"You warm enough?" Jordan asked as he walked over and squatted down to look more closely at him. Jason pulled the blanked up around his shoulders. "Yeah, I'm OK."

His eyes searched Jason's face for some sign that he wasn't being honest with him. "Listen, I need to go out and find more wood. I don't want that fire going out. Will you be OK if I leave for a while? How's your head and leg feeling?"

Jason grinned wickedly. "I don't 'feel' with my head or leg. I feel with my fingers." He laughed at his own joke but suddenly stopped, gritting his teeth with pain. "I'll be OK. Go ahead and do what ever you have to do."

Jordan reached out and gripped Jason's hand. "Hang in there, Jason. I know they're looking for us. Just rest, I'll be back as soon as I can."

Jordan glanced at his watch. 1:30 am. Quickly he stuck his ax thru a loop on his jacket, grabbed his flashlight, and left the cave. He made several trips back to the cave with armloads of wood and dumped them off to the side of the entrance, just inside the cave.

At 2:00 Jordan went out one last time to gather up smaller branches to supplement the larger pieces he had already put in the cave.

"Bill, where are you?"

"We're on our way. How's Jason doing?"

"His leg's broken. I had to put a splint on it. I found a cave about twenty-five feet south of where I went down into the ravine and I've moved him to it. I also have a fire going. He's in a lot of pain but seems to be holding up."

"I don't know if we will find you before morning. Do you think you can handle that?"

"Yeah."

"OK, just try to keep the fire going, and we'll get to you as soon as we can."

"OK."

Jordan dumped the smaller pieces of wood on the ground next to the fire and went over to Jason. The air in the cave was actually feeling warm and comfortable. "How you doing, are you hungry?"

Jason looked up at him with feverish eyes. "I thought you didn't want me to puke on you? I am a little thirsty." He held up the empty water bottle.

Jordan went over and picked up his pack, threw another couple pieces of wood on the fire, and came back over to Jason. Plopping down on the ground beside him, he got another water bottle out of his pack and handed it to him. He reached into his pack again and pulled out an apple. He paused, looking at Jason. "Will it make you sick if I eat this?"

Jason wiped his mouth after taking a big swig of the water. "No, go ahead." He capped the water bottle, then leaned his head back again and closed his eyes.

Jordan chewed on his apple, looking at Jason. "How's the

head feeling?"

Jason did not move. "It's throbbing."

Jordan got on his knees, set the apple down, and pulled a smaller flashlight from the outside pocket of his jacket. "Open your eyes; I want to see if your pupils are still dilating properly."

Jason obediently opened his eyes for Jordan to check them. Satisfied they were OK, Jordan sat back down. "They seem OK, but I don't know if I should let you go to sleep or not." Jordan took another bite of his apple and turned to look at Jason. "OK, I'm going to talk to you to try and keep you awake. If you do fall asleep, I will have to wake you up at least every half hour. OK?"

Jason smiled. "Yeah, OK. Thanks, buddy."

CHAPTER TWENTY-FOUR

BONDING

Bill, Sally, Angelina, and Chief Waits met up with Mr. Allen, Travis, and Austin at the three forks in the trail where the boys and Mr. Allen had originally split up. It had taken them a good forty minutes to reach the second stopping point. The moon was much lower in the sky and more clouds now hid many of the stars.

Mr. Allen explained that he had waited at the campsite for thirty minutes before he had gone looking for Travis and Austin. They too had gotten lost, but had not suffered the same fate as Jordan and Jason. Mr. Allen eventually found them and led them to the campsite where they had waited for another thirty minutes. When Jordan and Jason did not show up they returned to the three forks point to see if the boys had returned there.

Travis and Austin had set up the tents, and there was a nice fire blazing. Mr. Allen offered them hot chocolate to drink while they let the horses rest. Travis and Austin were sitting by the fire trying to stay awake. Chief Waits went to talk to them.

Angelina walked over to the left fork trail and scanned the ground with her flashlight. Bill and Mr. Allen were talking quietly, looking at the map Mr. Allen had spread out on a log. Sally had been listening to what Mr. Allen was saying, but looking over and seeing Angelina anxiously searching the ground she walked over to her.

"Angelina, you're upset you can't hear Jordan or reach him, aren't you?"

Angelina kicked at a rock, sending it flying into the brush. "He could hear me yesterday without touching; why can't he now? Why can't I hear him? Is he OK?" Angelina's voice shook with fear and frustration.

"You are just learning to develop that ability, Angelina; you are a long distance from him, and don't forget, you are both under a little stress right now."

"A little stress? I'm really scared, Sally. What if something should happen to him? I don't know if I could take losing him!" Angelina stood staring at Sally, tears in her eyes, not even realizing she had said "Sally" instead of "Mom."

Sally looked sadly at Angelina. She reached out and brushed some of the loose hairs from her ponytail out of her eyes. "Life isn't fair or easy, Angelina, but every moment we have is worth whatever price we have to pay."

Bill walked up to them. "I just spoke with Jordan. He told me Jason's leg is broken. He managed to get it splinted; he found a cave and has a fire going." Bill reached out with his thumb and wiped a tear off Angelina's cheek. "It's almost 3:00. Mr. Allen thinks we should try to rest and then head out at first light." Angelina started to protest the wait, but Bill continued. "He's pretty sure of the general area they are in but feels it would be safer to search at daylight."

Angelina stood staring at Bill. He reached out and gently

touched her arm. Suddenly she could hear Jordan. *"We're OK, Angelina; trust Bill. I'll see you in a few hours. Try to get some rest."*

With tears streaming down her cheeks, Angelina nodded at Bill. "OK, Bill."

The three of them walked over to the horses to get their bedrolls. Austin and Travis were talking to Mr. Allen. As Mr. Allen turned toward Bill, Travis and Austin headed for one of the two tents and climbed inside, closing the flap behind them.

Mr. Allen smiled at Sally and Angelina. "Why don't you and Angelina take the other tent? Bill, James, and I will stay out here and take turns keeping the fire going."

Sally smiled back at Mr. Allen. "Thanks, George." She gently guided Angelina to the tent. It only took a few minutes to roll out their bedrolls, and soon they were both lying on their backs, trying to relax enough to go to sleep. Angelina turned on her side away from Sally as her eyes filled with tears, her mind in a turmoil from all the emotions she was feeling.

She had been quietly crying for almost ten minutes when Sally sighed softly, and, getting up, moved her bedroll over next to Angelina. She lay back down and then slipped her arms around Angelina, drawing her close. Angelina turned and buried her face in Sally's shoulder, continuing to cry softly.

"There, there Angelina," Sally whispered lovingly. "Everything's going to be OK, honey."

Angelina looked up at Sally. "You said life isn't fair, but the rewards were worth the price. What did you mean by that?"

"Hard times, bad things, happen to both the good and the bad. We can choose to be bitter about this fact, or we can pull ourselves up by our bootstraps and choose to keep trudging on and always believe the best."

Sally paused, gently stroking Angelina's head. "My parents died when I was just seven years old, Elizabeth was only five. They were killed when part of the barn roof caved in. Elizabeth was beautiful, wonderful, full of life and wonder at all we could do. My sweet Elizabeth ran away when she was fifteen. A year and a half later, Grandma and Grandpa were killed in the fire when our home burned down. I lost my whole family, everyone. Then I met Bill. Even though we never had children, we were happy and content. Then Bill heard about you from the county social services office. We knew the moment we saw you, all scared and nervous, that you belonged with us. Now, knowing that you are actually my sister's little girl, well, the reward has been worth the price."

Sally looked down at the now relaxed and sleeping Angelina. She felt the tears slipping down her own cheeks. *"Well worth the price!* Sally smiled at Bill's silent echo. *"Amen!"*

~

Jordan woke with a start. The fire was low, so he got up and carefully put more wood on the glowing coals, blowing gently till the dry pieces of wood started to burn. Quietly he walked over to Jason. Reaching out he shook Jason's shoulder. "Hey, Jason, can you wake up a minute?"

Jason moaned softly and slowly opened his eyes, looking directly at Jordan. "What's up, man? Did I fall asleep?"

"Yeah, we both did, I think. I just put more wood on the fire. You warm enough? Can you let me check your eyes? How's the head and leg feeling?" Jordan checked the bandage on Jason's left leg. The bleeding seemed to have stopped; that was good sign.

"I'm warm enough, I guess. My head and leg both still hurt though." Jason chuckled. "Sure, Doc, you can check my eyes; check to your heart's content."

~ CHAPTER TWENTY-FOUR ~

Jordan checked his eyes; the pupils still seemed OK, but Jason felt warm to the touch. Jordan picked up the water bottle and handed it to Jason. "You feel like eating anything?"

"Got a T-bone steak in that pack of yours?" he asked before taking a drink.

"No, but I do have some bread and peanut butter."

"Sounds like a feast to me."

Jordan cleaned off his knife with a little water, spread a slice of bread with peanut butter, folded it in half, and handed it to Jason. "Eat it slowly. We don't want it coming back to revisit us."

Jason took the bread from Jordan and took a small bite, chewing slowly. He watched Jordan make a sandwich for himself, and then asked, "What time is it?"

Jordan looked at his watch in the light from the fire. "It's 4:45; it should be light in a couple more hours."

Jason continued to slowly eat his slice of bread, watching Jordan wolf down his and then reach for another slice of bread. "So, did you figure out what pushes your buttons?"

Jordan looked up at him startled. "What?"

"You know, our assignment, what 'fuel' affects you? Is it different with different people, oh, excuse me, with different 'relationships?'

Jordan was silent for a moment, focusing all his attention on the bread and peanut butter. He handed Jason the slice he'd prepared and then started on another one for himself. When it was fixed, he took a bite, chewing slowly, and finally looked up at Jason.

"I've been giving that assignment a lot of thought this past week. What you wrote for our Creative Writing assignment, well that really made me stop and think about it even more. It's true we do not have a lot of control over situations that happen to us. I'm beginning to understand that the control comes from how we choose to react to any given situation. I think we both know that some relationships are easier to deal with than others. But, given the right fuel, even the best of relationships can suffer damage depending on the choices we make and the actions we execute." Jordan paused to take a quick drink of water, and then continued.

"I guess the one thing I have learned since that most eventful day on the field when you, Travis, and Austin tried to beat the crap out of me is that believing in someone, even when things look bad, and holding on to hope, even when it seems like there is no hope left, well, miracles do happen!"

Jordan looked at Jason, who had been watching him closely. "And sometimes, there's more to someone than you ever imagined, and given a little time, and faith, even they will find themselves."

Jason reached out and grasped Jordan's hand. "Thanks for helping me to find myself, Jordan."

Jordan held his hand in a firm, friendly grasp, very much aware of the magnitude of the moment. "Oh, I think we helped each other, Jason; we helped each other!"

A real bonding had begun.

CHAPTER TWENTY-FIVE

THE RESCUE

Jordan had dozed off again. A low growl outside the cave startled him to full wakefulness. He looked over at Jason, who had fallen asleep too, but who was now also wide-awake. His eyes were large, and there was a hint of panic in his voice. "What was that?"

Jordan was on his feet in an instant. He reached over and picked a burning branch from the fire. Jason whispered, "Be careful!"

Holding the burning branch out in front of him, Jordan snapped his knife open with his other hand. At the entrance to the cave, he crouched down, straining to see where the growling was coming from. He glanced back as Jason tossed another piece of wood on the fire, making the flames leap high in the air. He looked back outside, moving the burning piece of wood back and forth; hoping to see if he could spot what he now thought must either be a wolf or a wild dog. He stopped moving, straining to hear. Off to the left of the cave he thought he heard some rustling sounds moving in a northerly direction.

Finally he stood up and walked back into the cave, tossing the burning branch back onto the fire. He looked at Jason's anxious face. "I think whatever it was has moved off. It's starting to get light out there. We should be OK if we keep a good fire going. I brought in a lot of wood, so we shouldn't run out."

Jason's expression started to relax. He nodded in agreement. "Sorry I'm no help, man."

Jordan tossed more wood on the fire. "Hey, except for you getting hurt, this has been a great adventure!"

Jason laughed. "Yeah right; well next time you can go off half-cocked and get hurt and I'll save your butt!"

Jordan grinned and then looked directly at Jason. "Next time?" Jason slowly raised his head. Jordan grinned broadly at him and shook his head. "I say next time we ride horses, neither of us goes off half-cocked, and we, you and I, we both save everybody else!"

Jason's face broke into a grin and he laughed, nodding at him. "I like the way you think, man. Now, you got anything besides peanut butter in that pack of yours?"

~

Angelina opened her eyes to see Bill poking his head in the tent flap. "Rise and shine; breakfast is almost ready. We're going to eat and then roll out of here in about twenty minutes."

Angelina scrambled out of her bedroll, pulled on her boots and then rolled and tied up the bedroll. As she crawled out of the tent she saw Sally over by the campfire with Mr. Allen, fixing something over the fire.

Angelina took her bedroll over to the horses. Bill had just put the saddle back on her horse. She secured her bedroll to the back of her saddle, rubbed her horse's nose, and then slipped into the bushes for a private moment.

When Angelina got back to the campfire, Austin and Travis were taking down the tents and repacking them. Sally handed her a mug of hot cocoa and a tin plate of scrambled eggs and toasted bread. Angelina sat down on a log close to the fire and started eating while watching Bill, Chief Waits, and Mr. Allen again look over the map, discussing the direction they should go.

Sally filled two plates for Travis and Austin, and then turned and walked over to them.

Angelina set her plate down. *"Jordan? Jordan, can you hear me?"*

"Angelina? Where are you?"

"We're at the fork in the trail where you all split up last night. Are you OK? Is Jason alright?"

"I'm OK. So is Jason. He's dozing right now. I've had to keep waking him up all night, every forty-five minutes to an hour, because of his concussion. I don't think it's too bad, but I didn't want to take a chance. I'm more worried about his broken leg. I cleaned the wound with water after I reset the bone, but I didn't have peroxide to really clean it, so I'm worried about infection."

"How far do you think you are from the fork?"

"We walked for about twenty minutes before we came to the second fork in the trail. We took the right fork and then walked for probably another forty-five minutes before Jason decided to go cross-country to try and get back to the correct path. We twisted and turned so much that I'm really not sure where we are. I do still have a fire going. I'll put more wood on so that you can see the smoke."

"Put one piece of damp wood on the fire if you have it; that should make some smoke that we can see."

"OK. So, are you OK? Did you sleep any?"

"I guess I'm OK. I was really worried about you and Jason! Sally and I shared a tent. I slept a couple of hours. How about you?"

"I slept a little, till we had a visit from either a wolf or wild dog. The fire kept him away, but I haven't slept since then, wanted to be sure the fire didn't go out."

"OK, well, we're ready to leave now. We'll see you soon!"

Angelina hurried over to the horses with Sally and mounted her horse. Bill helped Sally up and then mounted his own. Mr. Allen finished talking with Travis and Austin then came and mounted the horse they had brought with them for him. As Mr. Allen led them off up the trail that Jason and Jordan had taken the night before, Travis and Austin stood watching till they all disappeared from view. Then they turned and started the hike back to the Allens' farmhouse.

They followed Mr. Allen single file up the trail, Bill behind Mr. Allen, Sally behind Bill followed by Angelina, with Chief Waits bringing up the rear. The morning air was chilly, but the clear blue sky promised another nice late Indian summer day. Every now and then a bird would rise into the sky from the brush or a squirrel would run chattering up a tree. Twice they saw deer moving through the trees, always keeping a good distance between them.

They reached the second fork after ten minutes of slow riding. Instead of taking the right fork, like Jason and Jordan had the night before, Mr. Allen led them up the left-hand trail. They rode for another ten minutes before Mr. Allen took them off the trail and they continued on through the woods in a northwesterly direction. After another thirty minutes of very slow riding, Mr. Allen turned them on a southwest heading, and soon they came to a ravine.

Suddenly Angelina called out, standing up in her stirrups, pointing off to her left, "Look! There's a rope tied to that tree!" She was off her horse and to the edge of the ravine almost before the others could stop and look to where she had been pointing.

"Be careful, Angelina!"

The others turned around and came back to where Angelina was looking down into the ravine. After securing all the horses they rigged another rope, and soon Bill and Chief Waits were climbing down into the ravine. They could now see the smoke from Jordan's fire, and Bill and Chief Waits were able to reach them minutes after reaching the bottom of the ravine.

Forty-five minutes later, both Jordan and Jason were topside. Angelina fussed to Sally, *"If we were by ourselves and Jason was unconscious, we'd have him up in a second!"* Sally laughed softly at Angelina's frustration and Jordan's grateful sigh at not having to *float* up out of the ravine. Once Chief Waits had secured the tram poles to his horse, they settled Jason comfortably on the tram and prepared to make the long, slow ride back through the woods to the trail.

Chief Waits walked beside his horse to better lead it around boulders and fallen trees, trying to keep Jason's ride as comfortable as possible. Jordan and Angelina rode together on her horse. Jason never complained once but joked with Jordan and Angelina the entire hour-and-a-half trip back out to the campsite of the night before.

When the campsite came into view they could see Travis and Austin climbing on one of the big boulders. Mrs. Allen was standing beside the Land Rover, watching for them. Travis and Austin started yelling and came running to meet them.

It did not take them long to get Jason comfortably settled in the SUV. Angelina stood holding the reins of her horse and the one Chief Waits had rode, watching Jordan talk to Jason. They laughed and then grasped hands. Jordan then turned to Travis and Austin, and the three of them pounded on each other for a moment before

Travis and Austin climbed in with Jason.

Bill and Mr. Allen had taken the tram apart and repacked it. Chief Waits secured it to the top of the Land Rover, he got in the front with Mrs. Allen, and they headed back toward the farmhouse.

Jordan watched them drive away. Mr. Allen came up to him and put his hand on his shoulder. "You did a great job, Jordan. I'm sure Jason is going to be just fine. June called Dr. Johnson when Travis and Austin got back to the farm this morning. He will be waiting for Jason and Chief Waits when they get to town. Come on, let's mount up and head for home."

Jordan turned to walk over to the horse that Chief Waits had been riding with his head ringing. *"You really did do a great job, Jordan. We're so proud of you!"* Jordan grinned at Angelina as he swung up into the saddle.

CHAPTER TWENTY-SIX

A STARTLING DISCOVERY

It took them thirty minutes to ride back to the farm. Chief Waits was just pulling away with Jason. Travis and Austin were standing on the porch with Mrs. Allen.

As everyone unloaded their gear onto the front porch, Mrs. Allen invited Bill and Sally in for coffee or hot chocolate, and fresh cinnamon rolls. As she turned toward the door, she looked over at Travis and Austin. "Well, what are you two monkeys waiting for? You've been drooling over those cinnamon rolls ever since you first got back this morning, so I guess you've waited long enough. Go on in!" The boys tore past her into the house.

Bill and Sally looked at Jordan and Angelina for a moment, then turned and went into the house. Mrs. Allen stood in the doorway, looking at her husband. A slow, warm smile spread across her face. Mr. Allen smiled back. "We'll be back in a few minutes. Jordan and Angelina are going to help me with the horses." Mrs. Allen nodded, smiling, and went inside, shutting the door behind her.

Mr. Allen and Jordan each led two horses down to the barn. Angelina followed, leading her horse. The horses went into the respective stalls almost without guidance. The three of them worked together removing the saddles, brushing the horses down, and then getting them pails of water and fresh hay.

As Mr. Allen put the pitchforks away, he turned to Jordan and Angelina. "I want to thank you two for helping me take care of the horses."

Jordan grinned. "No problem, Mr. Allen. It's the least I could do. I'm really sorry for all the trouble I caused on the hike. I guess it didn't turn out the way you planned."

"The trouble *you* caused?" Mr. Allen stood looking at Jordan, a slight smile twinkling in his eyes.

"Well, Jason and I, together." Jordan had stuffed his hands into his jean pockets and was staring at his feet.

Mr. Allen continued to look at Jordan in silent contemplation. "Jordan, do you think we accomplished what we set out to do?"

Jordan slowly looked up at Mr. Allen. Finally he said, "I think we accomplished more than we had originally hoped for, Mr. Allen. Not only has Jason changed, but so have I. I think that Austin and Travis are coming around, but I know for sure things will be different from now on between Jason and me."

Mr. Allen nodded, smiling. He looked at Angelina, as if he thought she might want to say something. Angelina looked down, scuffing her foot around in the straw on the floor. *"How can I tell him how all of this has changed me too, without letting him in on my secret?"*

She looked up as Mr. Allen spoke. "Well, you two go on up to the house. I can hear your bellies calling out to those cinnamon rolls Mother made. I'm just going to lock up, and then I'll be right up."

~ CHAPTER TWENTY-SIX ~

Jordan and Angelina both said thanks, and taking hold of each other's hand, headed out of the barn. Jordan glanced over at Angelina. *"I can't believe how all of this turned out! It's amazing!"*

Angelina shook her head. *"Who'd of thought it would all work out so well?"*

"Jason and I were really starting to connect, but these last few hours alone with him, getting through this experience, well, I think it just cemented things for us."

As they reached the gate, both Jordan and Angelina stopped dead in their tracks and turned to stare at each other as Mr. Allen's voice came loud and clear into their minds.

"Did you two ever think that just maybe everything happens for a reason? Or that maybe it's all part of a much bigger plan, and that the overall effect will touch more than just you four boys, and you, Miss Angelina Beacon?"

Angelina turned slowly to look into the laughing eyes of her teacher.

Mr. Allen?

~

The End

Who's Who in "*Angelina Beacon Series*"
Listed alphabetically by last name (* Have same abilities as Angelina)

Jim Adams	Brother to Georgia Greene - lives in apartment above the Hair Salon.
Mr. Albert Aims	Teacher at Bakers Bluff High School; Political Science, and Public Speaking and 11th grade Study Hall teacher
Mrs. June Aims	Works at Bakers Bluff High School; School Librarian, Lunch room cashier.
Mr. George Allen*	Teaches at Bakers Bluff High School; European History, and Current Affairs, 10th grade Guidance Counselor & 12th grade Study Hall teacher.
Mrs. Bertha Allen*	Wife of George Allen; teaches at Bakers Bluff High School; Life Skills, and Introduction to Art.
James Allen*	Son of George & Bertha - missing for 17 years
William & Elizabeth Andrews	Parents of Travis and Katie; William owns the Andrews Mortuary
Katie Andrews	Twin sister to Travis
Travis Andrews	Sophomore - friend of Jason Morton
Miss Applebee	Foster parent for one hour to Angelina Beacon
Philippe Armone'	Teaches at Bakers Bluff High School; French 101 - 104
Joe Armstrong	Attorney
Jessica Armstrong	Joe's wife - works in his office
Charles Baker*	Owner of Baker's Books and Stuff - Great-Great Grandson of Jonathon Baker who town is named for.
Angelina Beacon*	Sophomore-15 year old - main character
Elizabeth	Angelina's mother (real name-Elizabeth

Beacon*	Eloise Browner) Died in car accident when Angelina was 5 years old
Joel Bolton	EMT
Ann Briemont	School Nurse at Bakers Bluff High; teaches Health Science 101 & 102
Richard Briggs	Owner of Bakers Bluff Dailey Times (newspaper)
Evelyn Bradford	Jordan Bradford's mother; works at Bakers Bluff Dailey Times; husband, Norm left them 5 years ago.
Jordan Bradford	Sophomore - 15 year old friend & neighbor of Angelina Beacon
Miss Annabelle Bruster	Mr. Campbell's secretary and school office manager
Mr. John Burns	Father to Marney, Greg & Jody; teaches at Bakers Bluff High School, General Biology, and Human Anatomy, and is 9th grade Guidance Counselor.
Heather Burns	Wife of John, mother to Marney, Greg & Jody; Librarian at Bakers Bluff Public Library.
Marney Burns	Sophomore – science wiz
Greg Burns	Senior – brother to Marney and Jody; plays football
Jody Burns	Marney & Greg's little sister, age 9
Alex Conner	Deputy
Mr. Lawrence Crawford	Teacher at Bakers Bluff High School; Algebra 102, Geometry.
Mr. Alex Campbell*	Principal at Bakers Bluff High School
Mrs. June Campbell	Teaches at Bakers Bluff High; Voice 101 - 104, & Drama 101 - 104
Mr. Mark Damon	Teacher at Bakers Bluff High School; Band/Orchestra.
Angela Damon	Wife of Mark-runs one of the Bed & Breakfast Inn's
Dennis &	Juniors – play football – twins – sons of

Denton Damon	Mark & Angela
Stan Doolittle	Janitor at Bakers Bluff High School, father of Melissa
Melissa Doolittle	Sophomore, friend of Angelina.
Miss Alice Fisher	Teacher at Bakers Bluff High School; English 101, and Creative Writing.
John & Georgia Greene	Wendy's parents; John drives school bus for Bakers Bluff High School, also teaches Shop Class, Applied Art, Advanced Art; Georgia owns & runs Georgia's Hair & Nail Salon.
Wendy Greene	Junior; cheerleader
Jon Guber	Pharmacist and owner of Bakers Bluff Drug Store
Rev. Duane & Jennifer Hill	Duane is pastor of Bakers Bluff Bible Church, wife, Jennifer, plays piano at church and gives private lessons, also runs Second Time Around Shop; parents of Abby, Bobby and Tina.
Abby Hill	Sophomore, Angelina's best friend
Bobby & Tina Hill	Abby's little brother and sister; ages 11 and 9.
Jean Hyde	EMT
Mr. Adam Jacobson	Teacher at Bakers Bluff High School; Algebra 101, and Trigonometry, and 9th grade Study Hall teacher.
Albert Jenks*	Town Veterinarian - also runs the animal shelter.
Elizabeth Jenks	Works with Albert at Jenks Veterinary Clinic
Ethan Jenks*	Senior - plays football
Albert Jenks, Jr.*	Junior - Science nut
Dr. Anthony & Jill Johnson	Amy's parents; Anthony Johnson, is head Dr at Bakers Bluff General Hospital, mother - Jill- nurse at Bakers Bluff General.

Amy Johnson	Sophomore - popular cheerleader.
Mr. Sidney Kimmel	Teacher at Bakers Bluff High School; Computer Science, MS Word & Business, twin brother of Jonathan.
Mr. Jonathan Kimmel	Teacher at Bakers Bluff High School; MS Excel & Business, and Accounting, twin brother of Sidney.
Anthony & Jan Masters*	Owners of local grocery store
Toby Masters*	Junior in High School – Plays in band
George & Ann Morton	Jason and Jill's parents; George owns the local gas station, Ann is a stay at home mom.
Jill Morton	Jason's older sister – junior – cheer leader
Jason Morton	Sophomore, tough guy, plays on football team
Bill & Sally Peters*	Angelina Beacon's foster parents, Alex-pet cat. Bill owns and runs the local auto shop, Sally works at a local restaurant.
Alan Peters*	Bill's brother, works in Bill's Auto Shop
Jake & Emma Peters*	Bill and Alan Peters parents.
Michael & Pamela Reed	Michael is an EMT, Pamela works at Bakers Bluff Public Library.
Tony Reed	Junior – Plays in the Band
Mr. Phillip Roberts	Teacher at Bakers Bluff High School; American History, and US Government
Mr. Adam Simpson	Owner of Bakers Bluff Cannery
Belinda Sidney	Owns Belinda's Clothing Shop
Miss Pamela Simms	Caseworker – Social Worker
Jonathan Thomas	Austin's dad – owns and runs Thomas's Hardware; Mother - Mary died of cancer one year ago.
Austin Thomas	Sophomore - part of Jason's group
Mr. Anthony Timson	Athletic teacher / coach for the boys at Bakers Bluff High School.

Mrs. Gail Timson	Athletic teacher / coach for the girls at Bakers Bluff High School.
Mr. Norton Tolin	School cook at Bakers Bluff High School and teaches Applied Accounting, & 10th grade Study Hall teacher.
Andrew Thompson* Richard Thompson* William Thompson*	Father - Andrew and son's - Richard & William Own and run Thompson's Meat Processing Andrew is a widower, son's never married
James Waites*	Police Chief
Barbara Waites	Wife of James
Mr. Richard Walters	Teacher at Bakers Bluff High School; Physical Science and Chemistry, and 12th grade Guidance Counselor
Phyllis Walters	Wife of Richard - works in the office at the Cannery
Jeremy Walters	Sophomore - in the Science Club
Cynthia Walters	Junior - cheer leader
Phillip Wheaton Ann Wheaton	Mayor of Bakers Bluff - head of city council Manages the Farmers Market
Mrs. Beth Williams	Teacher at Bakers Bluff High School; English Lit and College Writing, & 11th grade Guidance Counselor - widow